CLUB TIMES

For Members' Eyes Only

Which Carson Has Been Playing in the Wainwrights' Sandbox?

I'm not pulling a fast one over on you, members. One of our elders saw some, ahem, *cozy* behavior between a certain Carson cowboy and a "bookish" Wainwright female not too long ago. Now, I don't want to start World War III here, but I'm just saying that some Carson-Wainwrights sure ain't feudin'! The betting pool for which Wainwright and which Carson will take place in the Yellow Rose Café after the lunch shift this coming Sunday. We hope you understand that this is all in good fun, members. We don't want to aggravate Archy Wainwright's ticker or Ford Carson's cholesterol count.

As usual, we're holding our candlelight vigil for valuable member Luke Callaghan's safe return from wherever he is. The little scamp is probably in some hot air balloon wafting over Japan, with a harem to boot! Phone home, Luke!

Of course you know it's not our place to poke into anyone's affairs, but does anyone know why Carl Bridges has been so grouchy lately? He almost bit one nameless club employee's head off for pouring his coffee too slowly. We're not here to judge; it's just that we care about our members. On a related note, do y'all remember Carl Bridges's scallawag son, Dylan? Now there's a handsome buck who's always up to no good. Wonder what he's doing now....

As always, members, make your best stop of the day right here at the Lone Star Country Club!

About the Author

MARIE FERRARELLA

began writing when she was eleven. She began
selling many years after that. Along the way, she
acquired a master's in Shakespearean Comedy, a
husband and two kids [in that order]—the dog
came later. She sold her first romance in November
of 1981. The road from there to here has a hundred
and thirty-eight more sales to it, with a hundred and
twenty being to Silhouette. She's been fortunate
enough to have received several RITA® nominations
over the years, with one win for *Father Goose* [in the
Traditional Category]. Marie hopes to be found one
day—many, many years from now—slumped over
her computer, writing to the last moment...with a
smile on her face.

She found working on the LONE STAR COUNTRY
CLUB series especially fun since she originally
learned how to speak English by watching old
John Wayne movies on Channel 13 and has
loved Westerns and anything with a western
flavor ever since.

MARIE FERRARELLA

TEXAS ROSE

Published by Silhouette Books

America's Publisher of Contemporary Romance

Special thanks and acknowledgment are given
to Marie Ferrarella for her contribution
to the LONE STAR COUNTRY CLUB series.

 SILHOUETTE BOOKS

ISBN 0-373-61353-9

TEXAS ROSE

Visit Silhouette at www.eHarlequin.com

Printed in U.S.A.

Welcome to the

LONE STAR
L S
C C
COUNTRY
CLUB
EST. 1923

Where Texas society reigns supreme—
and appearances are everything.

The search for Baby Lena's parents continue—and
scandal spreads like wildfire through Mission Creek....

Matt Carson: Although he is the target of the
Wainwrights' wrath for ruining their daughter's
sterling reputation, nothing is going to stop this
spurned cowboy from reclaiming his true love.
Even if it means following her to the bright lights
of New York City.

Rose Wainwright: When her forbidden tryst with
her family's most hated enemy results in a shocking
development, Rose makes the ultimate sacrifice to
protect the man she cherishes. But the truth has a
way of coming out....

The Undercover Investigation: Is the Mafia behind
the anonymous threats that Haley Mercado's trusted
friend and secret cohort has been receiving? Residents
beware: the Texas underworld might be on the verge
of wreaking more havoc in Mission Creek!

THE FAMILIES

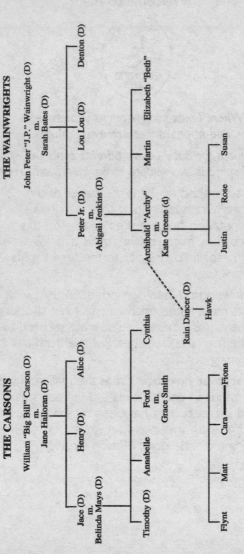

THE CARSONS

William "Big Bill" Carson (D)
m.
Jane Halloran (D)

Jace (D)
m.
Belinda Mays (D)

Henry (D)

Alice (D)

Cynthia

Ford
m.
Grace Smith

Timothy (D)

Annabelle

Flynt

Matt

Cara ━━━ Fiona

THE WAINWRIGHTS

John Peter "J.P." Wainwright (D)
m.
Sarah Bates (D)

Peter Jr. (D)
m.
Abigail Jenkins (D)

Lou Lou (D)

Denton (D)

Archibald "Archy"
m.
Kate Greene (d)

Martin

Elizabeth "Beth"

Justin

Rose

Susan

Rain Dancer (D)

Hawk

D Deceased
d Divorced
m. Married
----- Affair
_____ Twins

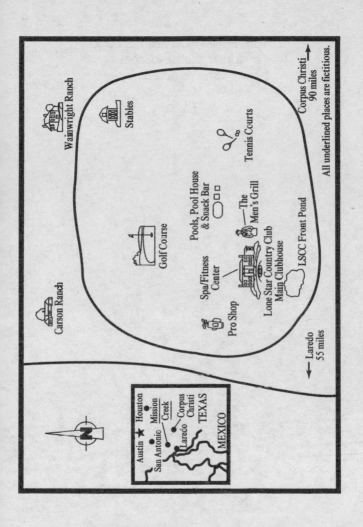

Wainwright Ranch

Carson Ranch

Stables

Golf Course

Pools, Pool House & Snack Bar

Spa/Fitness Center

The Men's Grill

Tennis Courts

Pro Shop

Lone Star Country Club Main Clubhouse

LSCC Front Pond

← Laredo
55 miles

Corpus Christi
90 miles

All underlined places are fictitious.

Austin ★   Houston
         Mission
         Creek
San Antonio   Corpus Christi
         Laredo
TEXAS

MEXICO

To Margaret O'Neill Marbury,
for all the headaches
she endured.
Love,
Marie

One

"Whose is it, girl?"

Archy Wainwright's question exploded like thunder, swallowing up the deathlike silence that had come a moment before. Stunned silence had been the initial reaction to Rose's quietly spoken announcement, delivered at the dining room table where her father, sister and brother had gathered for dinner.

The announcement had been an unwilling one on her part. If she'd had her choice, Rose Wainwright would have opted to spare her family the news altogether. Being told that his unmarried, thirty-year-old librarian daughter was pregnant wasn't exactly something a father wanted to hear—least of all the stern, volatile Archy Wainwright, respected land baron of one of the two oldest families in Mission Creek, Texas.

But it wasn't as if this was something that could remain a secret indefinitely. Even now, only six weeks along, Rose was certain she was going to begin showing at any moment. Despite her small waist. Despite the fact that her clothes still all fit just the way they always had. She *felt* pregnant. Hugely so.

Maybe it was the overwhelming weight of her secret that made her feel this way.

Or maybe it was because her world had been set on its ear ever since she'd stood in the bathroom within her wing of the sprawling ranch house, holding her breath, waiting for a small stick to decide her fate.

No, Rose amended, that wasn't really true. Her world had been upended ever since she'd first succumbed to Matt's charms and fallen in love with him. Ever since she'd first laid eyes on him. He'd leaned over the library counter and asked, with that devil of a twinkle in his beautiful blue eyes, if he could take out anything he found within the library. When she'd answered a tentative, "Yes," he'd put his hand on hers and said that what he really wanted to take out was the librarian.

Rose remembered blushing to the roots of her jet-black hair. Even so, she'd taken exception to Matt's unabashed flirtation. She'd been schooled to be cautious because he was, after all, who he was. A Carson. The enemy. Forbidden fruit.

At least, for a Wainwright girl. Or a Wainwright woman, as she now most definitely was.

Where had her mind been? she upbraided herself, watching as her father's complexion turned from mildly ruddy to deeply red. What could she have possibly been thinking, falling for Matt Carson? Making love with Matt Carson? Was she completely insane?

Yes, yes, she was, Rose thought. Completely and

utterly insane. Insane about him. But that didn't change anything. Not the situation, not the outcome. She, a Wainwright, was pregnant by a Carson.

And nobody was ever going to find out that part.

Standing in her bathroom, she'd dropped the stick into the trash can, crumpled to the floor herself and cried her heart out. Then she'd placed her hand over her too flat belly and wept some more for the child who was to be born. The child she already loved.

Even though she couldn't hide the fact that she was pregnant and becoming more so with each passing tick of the clock, Rose was determined to protect those she loved by not telling them who the father was. *All* those she loved, including Matt. It would only add to everyone's grief.

Not telling meant withstanding her father's tongue-lashing. It meant enduring the stony stare of her older brother, Justin, who also just happened to be the sheriff of Mission Ridge, the small town that the vast Wainwright ranch bordered. It meant withstanding her younger sister Susan's incredulous look.

But there was no other way. She had already made up her mind to have this baby. Alone. Telling her own father that her baby's father was Matt Carson would unleash a torrent of trouble that could only be equaled to the tumultuous origins of the feud that had separated the two once-friendly families and placed them on opposing ends of everything for the past seventy-five years.

Because it was unthinkable for a Carson and a Wainwright to actually entertain the idea of marriage, she deliberately hadn't told Matt that she was carrying his baby. She'd been afraid that he'd do something stupid, such as marry her because of the baby and estrange himself from his family. It was a guilt she felt unequal to bearing.

And worse still, she'd been afraid to tell him because she couldn't bear the thought that he might turn his back on her and tell her she was on her own. That getting pregnant was her fault, despite the precautions she'd taken. It was better to suppose, but not have the actual confirmation.

Though the thought of bearing Matt's child had drawn her closer to him emotionally, she had gone out of her way to instigate an argument that had led to the end of their clandestine affair.

Remembering that day, the day she'd broken it off, was painful. She'd lied for the first time in her adult life and told Matt that she wasn't excited by the thought of being with him any longer. That she was bored of it all and of him.

The words had tasted bitter in her mouth. Bitterer still had been enduring the look she'd seen in his eyes. His beautiful blue eyes had pain in them. Pain she had put there.

But there had been nothing else for her to do.

Rose clenched her hands in her lap as she stared

up into the face of the first man she had ever loved: her father.

Archy rubbed his chest in small, concentric circles, his eyes pinning her to her chair, as if willing his daughter to answer.

"Well?" he demanded when she made no response. "Who's the tomcat who's been sniffing around your skirts, girl? What's the name of the man whose hide I'm going to nail to the barn door?" His eyes became small slits beneath his bushy eyebrows. "Out with it, Rosie. I'll make him wish he was never born."

She lifted her chin. She'd always been a dutiful daughter, but that didn't mean that her spine had the consistency of wet spaghetti. She was, above all else, her father's daughter and could be just as stubborn as he was. "No."

"No?" Archy thundered in stunned disbelief. Rose had never been this blatantly defiant before, never challenged his authority.

Susan and Justin exchanged looks, waiting for the inevitable fallout.

Archy stared dumbfounded at his firstborn daughter. It had been only yesterday that he'd held that tiny, fragile little life in his large hands, amazed that something so tiny had such a will to live. Rose Ann Wainwright had been a preemie, born two months before she was scheduled to appear. The doctor had given her only a fifty-fifty chance of surviving the first forty-eight hours.

His Texas Rose had fooled them all. She'd not only lived, but thrived. Rosie was the quietest of them all, but he had always known there was a vein of stubbornness beneath the quiet.

Still, she'd been obedient to a fault, and he had to secretly admit that he liked it that way. This refusal to answer was the last thing he would have expected from her. The rebelliousness he saw in her eyes took him completely by surprise.

Surprise gave way to anger. "What in Sam Hill do you mean, 'no'?"

Rose clenched her hands harder. This was for everyone's good, she kept telling herself. She had to stay strong, had to refuse to give up Matt's name.

"Just that. No." She raised her chin, aware of the fact that her brother and sister were staring at her as if she'd suddenly turned into a giant condor right in front of their eyes. Her voice gained strength and volume as she continued. "No, I won't tell you who the father is. No, I won't be marrying him. And no, I won't let you bully anyone in my name."

"*Our* name, girl, *our* name," Archy reminded his daughter heatedly, his eyes as dark as the sky just before a Texas twister. "You're not some mongrel puppy, you're a Wainwright. Damn it, girl, that means something around here."

She refused to look away, even though she wanted

nothing more. But now wasn't the time to be a coward. She had to stand her ground. For her baby's sake. And for her father's.

"I know that, Dad."

Archy struggled to control his outrage and his pain. "No, I don't think you do. If you did, you wouldn't have gotten yourself in this state." With effort, his voice softened as he looked at her. "Are you sure, girl? You look so damn thin. Maybe it's just a mistake. You know, with the calendar."

"No," she replied quietly, "it's not a mistake with the calendar."

Rose watched her father's face fall. She knew she was taking away his last line of defense, his last hope. The euphemistic way he attempted to tiptoe around the delicate subject of monthly cycles touched her. Ordinarily her father had the finesse of a wrangler. If Archy Wainwright couldn't rope it and brand it, he couldn't deal with it.

But in his own clumsy way, he was trying.

And in his own clumsy way, Rose knew her father loved her. No matter how much fire he breathed and how loud he got. He didn't know how to show affection, only unadulterated anger.

Archy's face fell a full two inches. "Then you really are—?"

Her heart ached for him and if she could have gotten around the truth, she would have. "Yes, I really am."

Archy felt numb from the top of his head to the bottom of his toes. Numb, like the time his brother had accidentally dropped his rifle and shot him in the hip and shock had set in. "And you're keeping it?"

The question was half-rhetorical—because he was fairly confident that she wasn't the kind to simply wash away a life—and half stunned that his baby, his daughter, was carrying another man's seed. An unknown man at that. It took his very breath away.

Rose raised her eyes to her father's face without saying a word. She didn't have to. The look in her eyes said it all.

Archy blew out a long breath in frustration as diverging thoughts in his mind warred with his heart. How did he keep her protected from damning public opinion now that she'd gone and done this?

"Good," he barked, "because that's a life you've got inside you and it's half a Wainwright. But it's the other half I'm concerned about. Why won't you tell me who the father is, girl?"

Rose felt like crying and screaming. Ever since this baby had been formed, her emotions seemed to have settled on a constant roller-coaster ride that refused to come to a stop.

"Because you'd kill him and then Justin would have to arrest you," Susan spoke up, coming to her older sister's defense.

Under his breath Archy said something unintelligible and best not repeated. He waved an impatient hand at Rose, then looked at his son.

"Talk some sense into her, Justin. She's got an obligation to tell me who the young whelp is who did this to her."

He made it sound as if she'd been attacked instead of enjoying the most beautiful experience of her life. Rose felt the hair on the back of her neck rising.

"Did it ever occur to you that we did this to each other?" she asked evenly.

A fresh wave of thunder descended across her father's brow. "What did you say?"

There was a dangerous note in his voice and at any other time she might have backed off. But this time she had to take a stand.

"This is a love child, Dad." Her mouth was dry as she tried to make her point. "That means that the baby's father and I made—"

Archy quickly cut her off. "I don't want to hear it," he bellowed. "Besides," he scoffed, "what do you know about love? You've always got your head stuck in some book."

Justin laughed shortly. He'd always known there was more to Rose than his father gave her credit for. Still waters ran deep.

"Well, her head wasn't in a book at least one time," he commented. His father looked at him sharply. Trouble was definitely brewing and he was going to get caught in the middle. "Rosie, tell him who it is before he rides off into town with his twelve gauge under his arm, threatening to shoot every man above the age of puberty."

Rose pressed her lips together. There was no way he was getting the information out of her. For all she knew, her father could kill Matt with his bare hands. And then someone from the Carsons would kill him and so on, perpetuating the awful feud.

"It's my business, Dad. I'm a grown woman and I don't have to tell you if I don't want to."

Justin nodded thoughtfully. "She has a point."

Archy had expected support from Justin, not dissent. "She has a bun in the oven, boy, and that's a Wainwright oven," Archy bellowed. "I'm not going to become the laughingstock of the county, with people whispering about us behind our backs."

Susan rolled her eyes. Her father was too provincial for her to endure. "This is the twenty-first century, Dad. Nobody throws rocks at virgins who fall from grace anymore."

He looked at her sharply. "Stop right there, Suzy girl, or I'll have your brother lock you up in your room until you get so old, you'll be storing your teeth in a glass next to your bed."

This was going nowhere. Upset, Rose threw down her napkin and got to her feet, ready to run out. "You're impossible."

Her father rounded the table like a long-distance sprinter and headed her off. For his age and size, he was still surprisingly agile. He caught her by the shoulders before she could leave the room.

Justin was on his feet, ready to intervene if it came down to that. For now, he kept his peace.

"I'm head of this damn family and I still have a say in what goes on in it. Now tell me who this son of a bitch is who doesn't have enough guts to face me like a man."

She looked at his hands on either side of her. Suddenly aware of what he was doing, Archy dropped them to his sides.

Only then did she volunteer any more information. "He doesn't know."

Archy's mouth dropped open as he stared at her. "What is he, stupid?"

She felt very protective of Matt. "I didn't tell him."

Archy didn't understand her. In the world he dealt with, a man was supposed to pull his own weight and own up to his responsibilities. To do that, he couldn't be kept in the dark. Unless there was more to this than she was telling him. She *had* been abused, he thought suddenly.

"Why?"

She wished her father would drop this already. "That's my business."

"And what happens within this family is mine." He paused, gathering himself. Knowing that, at least for the time being, it was useless to keep hitting his head against a wall, he backed off. Just a little. "Well, I'm not going to have people flapping their jaws about you like you were common trash. You're going to live with my sister until this blows over."

"This isn't going to 'blow over,' Dad," Justin pointed out patiently. "Rosie's having the baby."

Archy waved a hand at his son. "Don't lecture to me, boy. I know that. That's just something I'll have to deal with later."

You're not going to have to deal *with it, Dad, I am,* Rose thought. But saying so out loud would only add fuel to the fire right now. She had to choose her battles.

"But Aunt Beth is in New York," Rose protested.

Archy loomed over his daughter, in no mood to put up with any more opposition. He'd endured all he was about to from Rose.

"So?" he demanded.

It was on the tip of her tongue to say that she didn't want to go to New York, but then Rose thought better of it. Maybe distance from everything and everyone was the best way for her to go right now.

Rose had remained under her father's roof all of her life. She liked being in the thick of things, close to those she loved, and had no desire to take flight the way so many others had. But now she couldn't go on living here with her father's accusatory looks. More important, she couldn't remain in Mission

Creek, running the risk of bumping into Matt when she least expected it.

If he saw her pregnant, there'd be no question in his mind that it was his. If he did do the so-called honorable thing and asked her to marry him, she might not have the strength to say no. And then there'd be a showdown between the two men she loved most: her father and Matt. That was something she definitely didn't want to have on her conscience.

"So I'll pack," Rose finally said. With that, she turned on her heel, leaving the other members of her family looking at one another in mute surprise and confusion.

"In a real short amount of time, Rosie's gotten to be a very contrary girl," Archy muttered more to himself than to the others at the table. "Even when she's doing what you think you want her to." He shook his head. "Just like her mother."

"What the hell's gotten into you?" Flynt Carson asked as he stormed into the stables. He looked at his younger brother, waiting for a response.

He didn't like the one he got.

Matt continued cleaning his tack. He'd been doing it for the past hour. It beat running his Jeep into the ground. Matt rubbed a narrow edge on the saddle. "Don't know what you're talking about."

Flynt glossed over the denial as if it'd never been spoken. He'd watched his even-tempered brother grow progressively surlier with each passing day for the past two weeks. Something was definitely going on.

"Hell, you never were a sweet-tempered kind of guy, but these days, if I were a stray dog or small child, I'd stay out of your way before you kicked me."

Matt snorted. "Wise thought." He stopped to pick up another cloth.

Flynt placed a hand on his brother's shoulder, forcing him to stop and look at him.

"Something's bothering you."

Matt knew Flynt meant well, but this wasn't something he could share. Not with any of them. He shrugged off his brother's hand and went back to polishing the tack. He was starting to wear the leather away. "Nothing I want to talk about."

Flynt repositioned himself so that he was in Matt's line of vision. "Maybe so, but the rest of us are getting caught in the fallout of that less-than-sweet disposition of yours and we're not going to take it for long."

Matt arched a brow in his brother's direction. "Then stay out of my way."

"Not always possible." As a rule, Flynt didn't meddle. But family meant bending rules. "Look, if it's about a woman—"

Matt looked at him sharply, the stilled cloth hanging in his hand. "What makes you think it's a woman?"

He'd hit a nerve, Flynt thought. The rumors about his younger brother and a so-called mystery woman were true, after all. Compassion nudged at him.

"I know the signs. Nothing like a woman to scramble up your insides worse than two eggs tossed into a blender. Way I see it, a fella's got only a handful of choices—you either marry her, put her in her place, or forget about her." And then, because the situation was a difficult one, Flynt added, "But do one of those things before the rest of us decide to form a lynch mob and put you out of our misery."

Matt tossed the cloth aside and sighed. "It's not that simple."

There was sympathy in Flynt's dark eyes. "I'm listening."

Matt was tempted, but he knew it would be a mistake. The affair had begun in secrecy and they'd both been aware of the consequences. "I'm not talking."

Flynt lost his temper. "Damn it, when did you get this obstinate?"

Matt bent to pick up the cloth again. He had to keep busy, even doing mindless chores. "Runs in the family."

"There's not going to be a family if we have to kill you." The smile faded. It looked as if his asocial brother had fallen and fallen hard. Why else would he be agonizing this way? This mystery woman of his had to be something else again. "Really, Matt, if it's serious enough to have you this chewed up inside, then maybe you should try to untangle whatever differences you've come up with and make peace with her."

Matt laughed shortly. "There's peace, all right. She dumped me."

Flynt looked at him, dumbfound. "Dumped you? You mean she has taste?" He slipped his arm around Matt's shoulders in a silent show of camaraderie. "Sorry, that just came out. Then maybe you're better off without her."

"That's what I've been trying to convince myself." And he wasn't getting anywhere. All he could think about was Rose.

"Haven't been having much luck, I take it?"

Matt sighed. "None at all. I think about her and my insides pinch."

Flynt nodded. He'd been at the same junction himself and knew how awful it could be. "That's either love, or you've been buying your underwear a size too small."

"Real nice, Flynt. Maybe the ladies church group will embroider that on some kitchen towels."

"Look, it's easy enough to confuse lust with that other L-word that's hard for us Carsons to say. Give it some time. If it's the first, it'll blow over. If it's the second, it'll get worse."

Matt's eyes met his brother's. "It already *is* worse."

He'd always been the straightforward one. "Then what are you doing sitting here talking to me? Go and tell her. Who is she, by the way?"

He didn't know if Flynt was being clever, or just asking. In either case, Matt couldn't tell him. He sighed and shook his head.

"Okay, don't tell me. But do something about it because, like I said, little brother, your days are numbered if you don't find that sunny disposition of yours again." Above everything, Flynt knew when to back off. He crossed to the stable entrance and then paused to add, "Just a word to the wise."

Matt said nothing. He was back to polishing his tack. And wishing he'd never set foot in that damn library and set his heart on the librarian. He should have stuck to cattle.

Two

"Well, good news, Harrison," Ben Ashton announced, sticking his head into the local district attorney's office after the latter had offered an absently voiced, "Come in."

D.A. Spence Harrison's relaxed demeanor immediately disappeared. The private investigator wasn't stopping by to exchange thoughts about a case coming to trial, he was here on a far more personal matter. A matter that had involved Spence and three of his closest friends, all because they'd had the unfortunate luck of being on the ninth tee of the Lone Star Country Club golf course the Sunday that the baby had been discovered.

Spence and his friends found the baby, crying and wet from a recent christening by the course's sprinkling system. The chance watering had inadvertently all but obliterated the note that had been pinned to the baby's blanket, a note that had, from all appearances, been addressed to the baby's father.

Because it was known that they frequently played at this time, they'd each been held suspect as the baby's father. The best way he knew of to eliminate suspicion, though, was voluntary DNA testing. Flynt Carson had decided that he needed to be the one to care for the baby. Child Protective Services had taken his DNA first and run it by a lab. Flynt wasn't the father.

Unwilling to have even a hint of scandal hovering over him, especially in view of his future aspirations, Spence had volunteered to be tested next.

Obviously, Ashton had the results in his possession now. He tried to read the private investigator's face, attempting to decide whether the smile there meant that the search had come to an end by some other means, or simply that his DNA test had been negative. He knew that there was no way on earth there was even a close match. This was not his baby.

Spence suppressed a sigh. He was due for some good news. He gestured to the chair in front of his mahogany desk.

Ashton shook his head. "Can't stay, Harrison. Just came by to tell you that you're not the baby's father."

Spence fixed the other man with a look. "I could have told you that."

"You did." The detective's reminder was droll. "But the police department likes to see proof and verify things for themselves."

Spence supposed that was what he and the others were paying this man for. To play the devil's advocate on their behalf as well as to find the identity of the baby's parents. He leaned back in his chair. "So who are you going to verify next?"

They both knew the answer to that. "With you and Carson in the clear, that leaves Tyler Murdoch and Michael O'Day."

Poor Michael, Spence thought. When they'd tapped him to fill Luke Callaghan's place to round out the foursome, the man had undoubtedly thought he was in for a morning of relaxation. With Luke away, gallivanting to places only the incredibly rich had the privilege to go to at a moment's notice, it seemed like an innocent enough thing to do. Michael hadn't known what he was in for. It could be that Michael O'Day just happened to be in the wrong place at the wrong time. Or not. Either way, things had to be done by the book. That meant checking out a man whose history with the group did not go back nearly as far as the rest of them.

When Ashton began to leave, Spence asked, "Want my prediction?"

The P.I. paused in the doorway, politely waiting.

"You're not going to find a match. You're wasting your time."

"But I'm not," Ashton pointed out. "We need to prove that none of you is the baby's father, that it was sheer coincidence that you found her when and where you did, at a time and place the four of you are known to be every Sunday." The detective smiled. "Besides, it's what you're paying me for."

Spence nodded. "Yes, I guess we are. Sorry if I sounded testy just then. This whole thing..." He waved his hand, letting the sentence just fade away. He couldn't put his restlessness into words. Spence looked back down at the brief he'd been reading when the private investigator had walked in. The meeting was over. "Keep me posted, Ben."

"Count on it."

The door closed firmly in his wake.

Spence reached for the phone to tell Tyler to expect Ashton soon. Instinct told him Tyler would be next on the investigator's list rather than Michael. It stood to reason. The man was trying to beat the police department to the punch and clear Tyler before any gossip via the news media took hold. Nothing the news media liked better than to find dirt sticking to a group of ex-combat heroes who'd managed to return from the Gulf War and work their way back into the civilian world, garnering money and prestige along the way.

Everyone loved a hero. And for some unknown reason, everyone loved finding tarnish on that same hero, Spence mused.

With a sigh, he began hitting the familiar keys on the keypad.

"So you've got everything you'll need?"

Rose stopped folding a blouse she knew she

couldn't wear much longer and turned around. Her father was standing in the doorway of her bedroom.

A tall, still athletically built man, Archy Wainwright looked a little lost for a moment, despite his stately stature. For a second she entertained a flashback. When she was a little girl she'd always thought of her father as being a giant of a man.

Too bad childhood didn't last longer, she thought sadly.

He'd shrunk a little in her eyes these past few months. Not because of any affliction of age, but because she knew how adamant her father was about the feud, a feud that had begun years before he was born and pitted their family against the Carsons on things that were only hearsay. The feud that was responsible for separating her from the man she loved.

If things had been different…

But they weren't, she told herself sternly, and she was strong enough to deal with that.

She hoped.

Rose dropped the blouse into the open suitcase. It was one of three spread out on top of her queen-size bed in various stages of being packed.

"Yes, I have everything."

Her voice was cold, Archy thought. He wasn't used to that. Not from Rose. He cleared his throat. "When are you leaving?"

"Tomorrow," she said crisply, as if they weren't discussing her exile but some short vacation from which she'd be back before her bed was cold. She paused, then added more softly, "I thought I'd go into Mission Creek and have a last look around when I'm finished."

Archy nodded. He wasn't a sentimental man, but he understood the need for it. "Need me to drive you?"

She didn't think that being with her father in close quarters for any length of time was wise right now. Besides, she wanted to be alone with her thoughts. Thoughts that involved Matt and the places they'd secretly met over the past few months. Months she intended to cherish despite the outcome of their affair.

"No. I can still drive."

Archy began to retreat, common sense telling him that it was best not to say anything else. But common sense gave way to filial passion. He wanted to make sense out of all this, and he couldn't.

"What were you thinking, girl? Didn't we enter into this at all for you?"

She straightened her shoulders, feeling under attack. "No," she replied simply. "You didn't. You don't govern my every waking moment, Dad. Just like I don't govern yours."

Archy's anger stirred. There was no comparing the two of them. "You're a child, I'm an adult."

In years gone by, just the hint of anger across her father's brow was enough to send her scurrying away. But she wasn't six anymore.

"Wrong, we're both adults and free to do what we choose." She raised her chin proudly, knowing she was doing the right thing. "And free to bear up to the consequences of those choices."

Archy resorted to an age-old defense. "You're breaking your mother's heart."

It took effort not to laugh at that. How could he throw her mother up to her, after what he'd done himself? Her mother had divorced him and moved out years ago because of his transgression and had only recently returned to care for her ailing mother. Kate Wainwright now spent part of her time living on the vast ranch in a small cabin her father had built for her.

"I suspect you took care of that long before I did." She saw her father's face turn red and knew he was struggling with choice words he didn't want to say to her. "See, I can play the guilt game, too, Dad. And it doesn't do either one of us a bit of good."

Like fire flashing in a pan only to be smothered by a lid, his anger dissipated, replaced by memories he didn't feel equipped to deal with at this time. He wasn't a man who liked to get sloppy. Archy took his firstborn daughter into his arms. "If you need anything…"

She understood what he was trying to tell her. Rose nodded, her soft hair brushing against his broad chest as she returned his embrace.

"I'll know who to call."

Afraid emotion would get the better of him, Archy left the room before either one of them could say another thing.

The bartender straightened the name tag on her blouse that proclaimed to anyone who passed through the doors of the Lone Star Country Club that she was Daisy. Daisy Parker was the name she'd taken to keep her own identity a secret until she could safely reveal who she really was. Those who mattered would be surprised to discover that beneath the dyed blond hair and the slightly altered appearance—thanks to a plastic surgeon in London—was a woman who had grown up among them as Haley Mercado. The same Haley Mercado whose family had ties to the Texas mob. The mob that was now after her.

Turning around, she went to take the order of the customer she'd heard come in. A woman, by the sound of the heels clicking on the Spanish tile.

Haley put on her brightest smile and walked up to the woman she recognized as Rose Wainwright.

"Why the long face, honey?" she asked in the deep Texas twang she'd affected.

Rose slid onto the stool and looked around the almost-empty room. "Just taking a last look around."

Haley cocked her head, hair that had once been a midnight-black but was now a golden blond brushing against her shoulder. "You going somewhere?"

Rose nodded and took a deep breath before saying, "New York."

She didn't sound very happy about it, Haley thought. "Business or pleasure?"

"A little bit of both." She laughed softly to herself. "A little of neither."

Haley saw her boss pass by the entrance to the lounge and nodded in his direction. Not twenty minutes ago he'd unwittingly enabled her to gather more information by asking her to tend bar for a big private party on Thursday night. The more she unobtrusively circulated, the more information the wire she wore would pick up. With any luck, the ordeal she was enduring would be over soon.

Haley felt rather bad that Rose's privacy was being invaded this way, but it couldn't be helped. The young woman did look as if she needed to talk. "So, what's your pleasure? The usual?"

Rose shook her head. "No. I'll just have a ginger ale."

The last two times she'd seen Rose, the older Wainwright daughter had ordered a white wine. Haley's brow arched. "That's even tamer than usual. Sure you don't want any wine?"

Rose shook her head. "I need a clear head."

Haley reached behind her on the bar, extracting a bottle of ginger ale. Twisting off the top, she poured the contents into a glass. "I've never seen you imbibe too much."

"Well, I've turned over a new leaf," Rose replied.

Haley set down the near-empty bottle. "New York and ginger ale. Any other new things?"

Rose pressed her lips together, seeming to be deep in thought.

"No, that's it for now." Rose wrapped her hand around the chunky glass that Daisy had placed in front of her on the counter.

"You don't look very happy about going."

She waved a hand. "I just have a lot on my mind."

This wasn't the kind of thing the FBI was hoping for when they wired Haley. None of what this unhappy young woman had to say would help her reach her own goal, that of reclaiming her life. But the sadness in Rose's eyes spoke to her.

She leaned forward, placing a hand on top of Rose's. "Honey, if you ever need someone to just listen, you know where to find me."

Rose smiled, obviously touched by the offer. "Thanks, but like I said, I'm going to New York."

"They've these newfangled things they call telephones. People talk into them and people on the other end can hear every word. Imagine that."

Rose laughed.

Haley smiled, her eyes crinkling. At least she'd done one good deed today. "That's better."

Matt finally understood the old, trite saying. He understood what it meant to be at wit's end, because he was at the end of his.

He had no idea what to do.

After deciding that Flynt was right, that he should take the bull by the horns before he allowed it to ram right through him, he'd gone to see Rose.

But she was gone.

She wasn't at the library, wasn't anywhere in town. And when he'd finally broken down and called her house, the woman who had answered the telephone informed him that Rose wasn't available. No details, nothing. Impatient, he'd asked when she would be back. The only answer he got was that information was unavailable at this time. Then the phone had gone dead.

He'd slammed down the receiver. What kind of garbage was that?

Unavailable.

That was the whole problem. Rose was supposed to be unavailable to him because he was a Carson. But she hadn't been. She'd been like fireflies and light. Magic. Pure magic in his arms, in his bed. The memory of making love with her into the wee hours of the morning clung to him tenaciously, coloring every moment of his day and night.

He couldn't go on this way.

Damn it, a man should be able to shake off anything, but he couldn't seem to shake off the effect she'd had on him. He needed to tell her that. To find her and talk to her face-to-face.

It couldn't just end like this, as if it hadn't meant anything.

It wasn't his ego that was at stake, it was his heart. Why couldn't she see that? She'd been so bright, so insightful about everything else, how could she not know what her leaving would do to him?

He'd tried to talk himself into believing that this had been just a fling, an affair. But it was a lie and he knew it from the start.

He needed a drink. A tall, stiff one.

Matt stormed into the Lone Star Country Club Men's Grill and planted himself on a stool at the bar. Because of the bomb that had gone off months earlier, the Men's Grill was under construction, forcing the patrons into temporary quarters.

He scowled into the mirror.

Amid a barful of customers, Haley saw him. Flynt Carson's younger brother. Flynt had been one of her brother Ricky's best friends before life had conspired against them and sent them in separate directions.

She made her way over to Matt, she on her side of the bar, he on his.

"Hi, handsome. A smile will really dress up that pretty face of yours."

Without asking, the bartender set a whiskey neat down in front of him.

Matt accepted the drink with a slight nod of his head. "Thanks, Daisy. But I don't have anything to smile about." Throwing back the contents of the shot glass, he set it down empty on the counter a moment later. "Hit me again."

Daisy reached for the bottle and poured. "Hey, go slow on that. Don't want to make extra work for the sheriff now, do we? What's the problem?"

He raised his eyes to hers. Suddenly he missed Rose's eyes. He cursed her soul to hell for what she'd done to him. "Nothing," he muttered moodily. "Everything."

"That about covers it." Haley watched him down the second drink and held off offering the third. At this pace, Matt Carson was working himself up for one powerful hangover.

"Yeah." He laughed without any humor. "I thought I had all the bases covered, too." He stared down at the empty glass—empty, like the way he felt. "But she fooled me."

"She?"

Matt nodded, hating this impotent way he felt. Where the hell *was* she? He leaned in over the counter, his voice low. The bartender was forced to lean forward to hear him.

"She's gone. I can't find her anywhere."

Haley thought back to the woman who had been in the Grill two days prior. With the same troubled look in her eyes. It didn't take a genius to make the connection.

"She?" Daisy asked. "That wouldn't be Rose Wainwright, now, would it?"

Matt looked at her sharply, then glanced around to see if anyone had overheard. Not likely, not in this din. "How did you—?"

Daisy's mouth curved in a comforting smile. "Don't worry, I won't say anything to anyone. I know all about that family feud of yours. Big waste of time if you ask me. But no one's asking me."

The hell with the feud, the hell with everything else except the woman who'd twisted his gut up so bad, it felt like a pretzel. "I'm asking you about Rose. Was she here? When? What did she say?"

The bartender nodded. "Day before yesterday. And she said she was leaving."

"Leaving?" Then he was right, she *had* gone. "Where did she say she was going?"

"New York."

"'New York'?" he echoed.

His first inclination was to say she had to be mistaken. New York wasn't the kind of place someone like Rose would go. But then he remembered. She had an aunt who lived in Manhattan. Beth Wainwright, that was her name.

Relief swept over him like a giant wave. Rose hadn't just disappeared into thin air. He knew where she was. And he was going to get her back. Grateful for the help, Matt leaned over the counter, took hold of Daisy's shoulders and kissed her soundly on the mouth.

"Thanks."

She pretended to fan herself. "Don't mention it." And then she winked. "Pleasant though that was, that doesn't take the place of a tip, you know."

Standing up, Matt pulled a twenty out of his wallet and tossed it onto the counter. "Keep the change," he told her. "And thanks."

For the first time in two days he knew where he was going.

The doorbell pealed incessantly, intruding into the mood that was enshrouding Rose.

Try as she might, she couldn't seem to shake loose of it. It hung about her like a coat of heavy iron malle. Her aunt had been nothing short of wonderful, insisting on taking her "fun" places, as she called them, and determined to make her smile. Rose tried her best not to show the older woman how deeply unhappy she was, but she had a feeling she wasn't fooling her.

She supposed that eventually the raging battle would die down to an occasional minor skirmish and Matt Carson would entirely cease to matter. In about a million years or so.

"Would you get that, darling? I have my hands full of caviar," Beth called from the kitchen.

Rose didn't even stop to ask. Her aunt's eccentricities were becoming normal.

Though she didn't feel like talking to anyone, she couldn't very well return Beth's kindness with surliness.

"Of course."

She supposed, she thought as she turned the lock and pulled on the doorknob, that she should welcome any distraction.

Except this one.

Rose's mouth fell open.

Matt Carson was standing in her aunt's doorway.

Three

Matt's was the last face Rose had expected to see in New York. For a split second she thought she was hallucinating. Her head and heart were so full of him that she thought she was just projecting his likeness onto someone else.

But he was real.

And he was here.

It took several beats to get her flustered heart under control. She willed herself to remain calm. "What are you doing here?"

The entire trip from Texas he'd rehearsed what he'd say to her, editing, augmenting, changing words up until the very last moment. Now that he was standing in front of her, his mind went blank and he said the first thing that came to him. The truth.

"Looking for you."

She wasn't going to fall into his arms, she wasn't. That would only set her back. She'd gone through this once, said goodbye and ended it. She wasn't up to dancing the same slow dance again.

"Well, you found me." She gripped the doorknob

tightly, ready to swing the door closed. "Now go away."

It was the wrong thing to say. He felt his anger, his hurt, flare up dangerously high. "I am *not* going to go away. Hell, woman, I've come over a thousand miles to talk to you."

He was standing there, looking better than any man had a right to. All she wanted to do was to throw her arms around him and tell him she was carrying his baby. Their baby.

Somehow, she found the strength not to.

"Then you wasted your time and your money because there's nothing to talk about." She squared her shoulders, doing her best to sound cold, but hating the way the words tasted in her mouth. Telling herself that it was all for the best was wearing very thin. "I said it all back in Mission Creek."

Matt's eyes narrowed. He struggled not to push his way in. He hadn't come all this way to frighten her, but he hadn't made the journey just to turn around and go home again, either.

"You might have said it all back there, but I didn't. I—"

He stopped as a petite, buxomy, dark-haired woman dressed in a black caftan with royal-blue dragons across it came to the door. Her heart-shaped face lit up as she looked at him, a twinkle shining in both dark eyes. "Is there a problem, dear?"

Her words were addressed to Rose, but her eyes

never left him. Matt felt as if he were being literally, smilingly dissected, inch by inch.

"My, my, my, who is this handsome devil?" The woman laughed softly, leaning forward, her hand on his arm. "If you're selling subscriptions, sign me up for a half dozen magazines. Better yet, why don't you come in and try to convince me to buy more?"

Oh God, no, Rose thought frantically, that was the last thing she wanted. "Aunt Beth, this is—" Rose stopped, feeling shaky inside.

It had to be the pregnancy, she thought in desperation, praying she wouldn't do something dumb like faint until after Matt was gone. Her head was spinning and she was struggling to keep the world in focus.

"I know who he is, dear," Beth said, managing to come off serene and flirtatious at the same time. She winked at Matt.

She'd had the complete story out of her niece within less than an hour of her arrival two days ago. Beth prided herself on getting people to talk to her, even when they were reluctant to do so. *Especially* when they were reluctant to do so. She firmly believed that secrets were best borne when they were shared. That went double for disturbing ones and she knew that this unplanned pregnancy had disturbed Rose's life greatly.

"With those beautiful blue eyes and that handsome, rugged face, he could only be one of Ford Carson's boys. Judging your age..." Beth cocked her head, pretending to scrutinize him, knowing that Rose would hate to have her divulge that she'd told her all about Matt and her delicate condition, a condition Beth knew he was completely unaware of. "I'd say you must be Matt."

Matt stared at the flamboyantly dressed woman at Rose's elbow. She looked to be exactly as Rose had once described her to be: one of those ageless women who had been everywhere, done everything. He knew that she was Archy Wainwright's older sister, which had to put her somewhere in her early sixties at the very least, but she wore her age well and almost seamlessly so. He could detect no wrinkles and only a few lines around her mouth, which Rose had once said Beth called laugh lines.

"Yes, I am."

"Well, don't just stand out there in the cold hallway, honey." Beth took a step toward him to pull him into the vast six-room Central Park West apartment. "Come on in and make yourself at home."

"He was just going," Rose insisted, looking at Matt for corroboration. She wished from the bottom of her heart that he hadn't come.

Was she really that eager to get rid of him? Was he just a poor, lovesick idiot wearing his heart on his sleeve for the first time? He had nothing to go by, no ruler to measure any of this with. He'd never felt for any other woman what he did for Rose. But it seemed to be one-sided, after all.

"Oh, but he can't go," Beth informed her sweetly. "He's only just now come." Calling an end to the discussion, Beth threaded her arms through Matt's, two heavy bejeweled hands crossing over each other to hold him in place. "Now come inside and take a load off those dusty boots of yours."

His arm held prisoner, Matt had no choice but to allow himself to be drawn into the apartment.

As he crossed the threshold, Matt looked around, slightly dazed. He had no idea that anything like this could exist in a city as crowded and noisy as the one he'd just walked through and left twenty floors below. The tremendous living room with its vaulted ceilings had modern furniture and an incredibly white rug that ran the expanse of the room. On the walls were framed photographs of Beth with celebrities and an assortment of husbands and several publicity shots from her acting career. He could feel the woman's vitality fairly leaping from every one.

Mindful of his boots, Matt looked down at the rug. It was as pristine as an untouched beach. "How do you keep it so white?"

The wink Beth gave him was nothing short of outrageous. He had a feeling the woman had been dynamite in her younger years, and probably still was a force to be reckoned with.

"You can manage anything with enough money, honey."

He didn't know about that. Money certainly wouldn't win him the woman he loved.

"Come." Beth coaxed him over to the ice-blue Italian leather sofa. "Sit."

Rose knew that Beth meant well, but this was getting severely out of hand. She looked pointedly at her aunt. "Aunt Beth, can I please see you?"

Making herself comfortable beside Matt, Beth looked up at her niece. "You see me now, dear."

Rose nodded toward the hallway beyond the living room. "In another room."

Matt inclined his head toward Beth. "I think she means without me."

Beth nodded. "I think so, too, dear. Always been a stubborn girl. But take it from me, she's worth waiting for." Rising, she patted his hand and then turned toward Rose, her caftan sweeping majestically. There was a patient look on her face. "All right, dear, I'm all yours. What room would you like to go to?"

"The den," Rose told her. The den, at least, had a door she could close. She didn't want her words being overheard by Matt.

Damn it, she was here as much to get over him as to spare her family any embarrassment because of her condition. Why did he have to show up and send her back to square one?

Who are you kidding? a small voice mocked Rose as she led the way to her aunt's den. *You're not anywhere near even started getting over him.*

She knew it was the truth. She hadn't really begun getting over him. But she didn't have a prayer of getting started while he was still here. To get rid of him, she had to get her aunt to stop trying to make him so comfortable.

Walking into the den, she waited for her aunt to cross the threshold before closing the door firmly behind her.

Beth turned around and looked at her niece patiently. In a gesture that was reminiscent of her theatrical days, she spread her arms wide. "All right, dear, here I am. What is it you want to say to me?"

Not for the world did she want to hurt her aunt's feelings. But Beth had to be made to understand. "I don't want you encouraging him to stay."

Beth laughed and shook her head. "He doesn't need my encouragement, dear. He's come all this way on his own." She sighed the way she did when she read the last page of a good romance novel. "Just to see you."

Agitated, frustrated, Rose began to pace. "But I don't want to see him."

Beth gave her a funny little look, becoming serious. Her voice was soft, almost hypnotic in its sincerity. "Yes, you do."

This was hard enough on her without having to argue about it. "Aunt Beth."

Beth had no children of her own, aside from a grown stepson by one of her late husbands. Gregory was in Chile on an oil rigger. She'd never had an opportunity to mother him, so she focused all that untapped motherly instinct on Rose.

"Give it some time, dear. Away from the others. There's a real spark between the two of you. I saw it the second you looked at each other. Hell, I *felt* it clear across the room."

Rose didn't ordinarily contradict anyone in her family, but her own need to survive had changed some of the rules. "You were in the other room the second we looked at each other," she pointed out.

As with most of her life, Beth shifted course to accommodate the current. "Like I said, I felt it. And the spark went on long enough for me to walk into the room." She took her niece's hand between both of hers, forcing Rose to look at her. "Sweetheart, don't let some silly feud that has nothing to do with either one of you ruin what could be a beautiful future."

Rose sighed, pulling her hand away. "It's not just the feud, Aunt Beth. And even if it was, it's not silly to my father."

Beth snorted, waving a dismissive hand. "Archy always was incredibly loyal to all the wrong things." She slipped a conspiratorial arm around Rose's slim shoulders, reaching up a little as she did so. Rose was a good three inches taller than her. "Darling, do you think that if the woman he loved was a Carson, he'd let some ancient feud stand in his way?" She laughed, remembering the man her brother used to be before stability and age had forced him to bury his wild streak. "Not when he was Matt's age. Your father was a hellion back then. If he'd fallen for a Carson—"

"But he didn't," Rose pointed out. "I did." And that made all the difference in the world.

Beth smiled from ear to ear, resting her case. "Uh-huh, see, you admit it."

The woman had tricked her, Rose thought. She might be eccentric, but that didn't mean Beth wasn't crafty. "Maybe," she partially conceded. "But that doesn't mean that I don't realize it's a mistake."

The look in Beth's eyes, as violet as Rose's, became dreamy as she remembered some of her earlier marriages and affairs.

"Love is never a mistake, dear. You're like Romeo and Juliet." She gave her a confident look. "Except you're going to have a happier ending."

Rose could have sworn Beth was making her a promise, but that was impossible. No one could promise that. She knew better.

"No, we're just going to have an ending," she said firmly. "Starting here and now."

Beth opened the door and was already beginning to walk away. "Can't hear you, dear. You must be talking into my bad ear."

Rose raised a suspicious brow. "You told me it was the other ear yesterday."

Beth turned toward her, unfazed. "These things have a tendency to switch, Rose, honey. You know how eccentric I am."

Moving quickly, Rose placed herself in front of her aunt. Beth wasn't going to leave the room until she promised not to interfere.

"Aunt Beth, do you remember the details of the feud?"

"Remember it?" She laughed. "It was drummed into my head almost every day when I was a child. I was ten years old before I realized it wasn't one of Aesop's fables."

Rose took hold of her aunt's broader shoulders to hold her in place. "All right, then, remember how Jace Carson proposed to the mayor's daughter just because he thought she was going to have his baby? He didn't love her, but he was ready to do the honorable thing."

Beth held up a finger, interrupting. "He didn't, though. The baby turned out to be the gardener's. The mayor's daughter was afraid her father wouldn't approve of him, so she kept it a secret until she couldn't contain it any longer, then blamed Jace. But everything turned out all right, except for poor Lou Lou." She'd always wanted to write a play about the feud and play the part of Lou Lou Wainwright, the woman who committed suicide when she found she couldn't marry her lifelong sweetheart, Jace Carson, and started off the feud.

Beth was straying off the path. Rose quickly redirected her attention to what she was trying to say. "The point is, Jace was going to marry her to do the right thing."

Beth looked at her niece, trying to second-guess her. "And you're afraid that if Matt knows, that's what he's going to do."

"Exactly."

Funny how two people could be in love, Beth thought, and still be so blind about the other person. It rather reminded her of the way she and Garrison had been about each other.

Beth quickly caught herself before her thoughts took her off in another direction.

"Not that I don't think your young man isn't honorable, dear, but I don't think anyone could make him do what he didn't want to do."

"That's just the point," Rose insisted. "He'd want to be honorable."

Beth cocked her head, trying to follow Rose's thinking. "And you don't want him honorable?"

"I don't want him marrying me to be honorable, or to give the baby a name." She swung around to face Beth as she made her point. "I want him to marry me because he loves me, because he wants a baby with me, not because he accepts me for his wife because I happen to be the mother of his baby. Do you see the difference, Aunt Beth?"

"Yes, I do. And if you don't think that that boy

loves you down to the soles of his worn cowboy boots, then you and I need to have a serious conversation.''

Rose held up her hand. ''No, no more talking. Please. I just want him to leave so I can get on with my life.''

Beth was thoroughly convinced that young people didn't know how to love these days. They kept insisting on getting in their own way.

''Now that I've had a gander at that boy, Rose, it doesn't seem like much of a life without him.''

Before Rose could launch into another argument, Beth left the den and swept majestically into the living room.

She beamed down at Matt, who immediately rose in his seat. Good looking *and* polite. She knew a great catch when she saw one. The thing of it was, to make Rose realize it, too.

''Sorry to leave you alone for so long, Matt.'' Beth saw that he'd opened the gold-bound book on the coffee table and had been leafing through it. She jumped at her opportunity. ''Oh, you've found my scrapbook.''

Nostalgia had her sinking down beside him on the sofa, ready to page through the book with him.

Only sheer will restrained Matt from doing a double take. The page opened in front of him was of an apparently nude, nubile woman who had strategically arranged feathers to cover all the important places. He looked from the page to Beth.

"This is you?" he asked.

"Yes." She was eighteen then and fresh from the ranch. It seemed like a million years ago now. And just like only yesterday. "I was on Broadway. Off-Broadway, actually. Way off." She'd worked her way up to the legitimate theater, and acquired many wonderful memories and almost as many men along the way. Beth sighed. "It's been a wonderful life." And then she smiled at Matt. "But you're not here to listen to me reminisce."

It occurred to him that he felt comfortable with this woman he'd never met before. As comfortable with Beth Wainwright Montgomery Cannon Williams Smith, et cetera as he was with Rose, or had been before she'd dumped him. Maybe it was a family trait, he reasoned. Although Rose was far less outgoing and flamboyant than her aunt. Truthfully, he was glad of that, because if she'd been like Beth, he would have had to stand in line instead of keeping her all for himself.

Matt sensed an ally in Beth and as such, felt that it was only smart to encourage her to continue. "No, please, go ahead."

Beth patted his hand, her violet eyes sparkling like newly uncorked champagne poured into a fluted glass. "Not just handsome, but smart, too." She laughed as she looked at Rose over Matt's head. "This one's a charmer, Rose."

"Yes," Rose said, looking pointedly at Matt. "But charm eventually wears thin."

The remark hit him straight in his heart, like a well-aimed arrow. What was he doing here, humbling himself in front of a woman who had walked out on him, who'd all but told him that she'd had her fun, but the excitement was gone and now it was time to return to their previous lives?

Where the hell was his pride?

"Since I'm here," he heard himself saying, "I might as well take a long overdue vacation. But this place is so damn confusing," he confided to Beth, ignoring Rose completely, "I'm going to need someone to be my guide." He waited for the offer he thought was inevitable. When it didn't come from Beth, he urged, "How about you? Are you up for it?"

To his surprise, Beth shook her head. "Oh, my dear, I would be more than up for it, but I'm right in the middle of teaching an acting class." Then she beamed as if suddenly struck by a thought that he suspected had been there all along. "But Rose is free."

He spared Rose a glance. "I don't expect she knows very much of the city."

"She knows a great deal more than you give her credit for, Matt."

He shifted in his seat, turning to look at Rose who was on his other side. Was it his imagination, or did she suddenly look pale? "All right, how about it? Will you show me around?"

Why were they playing these games? Why couldn't he just go home? "You don't really want to see the city," Rose replied.

Matt could feel his temper heating again. There was no doubt about it, Rose could set him off like nobody he knew.

"I said I did, didn't I? Why do you always have to contradict what I say?"

She was in no mood to be diplomatic. "Maybe it's because you never say what you mean."

Beth clapped her hands together three times before she managed to get their attention.

"Children, children, stop fighting this instant and make nice or I'll send you both to your rooms without any supper." A complete pushover, even in jest, she rethought that. "Well, that's too harsh, but without dessert at any rate." She winked.

Rose folded her hands in front of her and let out a deep breath. She supposed she had sounded like a child, arguing just now. And since it looked as if Matt wasn't about to leave unless she agreed to some kind of a tour of the city, she decided that this was the lesser of all evils.

"All right, I'll show you around the city if that's what you really want."

"I always love a warm invitation," he said sarcastically.

Beth intervened. "Make up and say yes, dear, before I show you your room."

Almost in shock, Rose stared at Beth and then Matt, praying that Beth was using some like of poetic license. "He's staying here?"

"Well, there was a suitcase in the hall next to his foot and I assumed it was his," Beth told her.

It could stay in the hallway for all Rose cared— along with him. "Just because he has a suitcase doesn't mean he has to put it here. This isn't a hotel." The moment she said it, she regretted it, knowing what was coming.

Beth didn't disappoint her. "No, of course not, but I took you in, didn't I?"

Rose tried to rally and dig herself out of the hole she'd fallen into. "I'm family."

Beth merely nodded sagely. Her near-death experience on the operating table several years ago had made her reestablish communication between herself and a higher power.

"We're all one big family in God's eyes, dear." She turned to Matt. "And Matt obviously needs a room, don't you, dear?"

He rose to his feet. "I was going to a hotel."

Leaning on the arm of the sofa, Beth pushed herself upright. "I'll save you the trouble. Third door on the left. Guest bedroom. I love having guests," she confided.

"Ms. Wainwright—"

"Call me Beth, please. And I won't hear another word about it. Keep arguing and you'll hurt my feelings. You wouldn't want to do that, now, would you?"

Matt shook his head in compliance, but Rose opened her mouth to protest. "But—"

"Good." Rose clapped her hands together. "Then it's settled. You're staying. It's a big apartment. We won't get in each other's way."

Unless, of course, I orchestrate something, Beth added silently.

Four

Rose was keenly aware that Matt was in the next room, settling in.

There was another guest bedroom on the other side of her aunt's room. Why hadn't Beth given him that one? Why the one next to hers? What was she trying to do to her? Rose thought moodily. It was hard enough dealing with emotions and hormones that were completely out of kilter because of her condition without having to put up with barbarians not only at the gate, but storming through those same gates, as well.

Matt had told Beth that he was planning to stay in New York about a week or two. He'd been looking at Rose when he'd said it, as if the length of time depended strictly on her.

If that was the case, he should be on a plane for home right now, Rose thought, frustrated.

Making up her mind to convince Beth to withdraw her invitation to Matt, Rose left her bedroom and went looking for her aunt.

Instead she ran into a mini army of people carrying covered dishes toward the terrace.

Following their path with her eyes, Rose found Beth. She was holding court on the terrace. Right in the middle of things, as always, stood Beth, pointing and issuing soft-spoken orders like a general mantled in a flowing caftan.

Rose stepped out of the way of a young, trim-waisted man in black livery carrying a small box. Feeling like someone in the middle of Atlantis moments before the fatal earthquake, she made a beeline for her aunt.

"Aunt Beth, what is all this?"

"Right there will be fine, dear," she said to the young woman with the salad bowl. Beth spared Rose a quick glance over her shoulder. "Why, it's dinner, darling. What does it look like?"

There were crystal goblets, a very fancy bottle of what appeared to be ginger ale, another of champagne. Covered entrée dishes sat atop a table graced with a cream-colored lace cloth and overlooking the park that dusk was slowly covering.

"Throwing a couple of steaks in the frying pan and tossing in a salad is dinner," Rose informed her. "This is a conspiracy."

Beth laughed and patted Rose's cheek. "Nonsense, Rose, there's no conspiracy." She leaned into her niece, lowering her voice. "You know, it's a known fact that some women in your condition start becoming paranoid."

Rose stiffened and turned around, looking toward

the living room to make sure that Matt wasn't anywhere in the vicinity.

"Aunt Beth—" she said between clenched teeth.
This was supposed to remain a family secret and here
Beth was, talking about it in the middle of a circus
of strangers.

Beth lowered her voice even more. "I'm whispering, honey. Even you can't hear me." She came to
attention as another man came out on the terrace with
a small, narrow box in his hands. "Oh, put that right
there. I'll take care of it."

Ignoring the crisis Rose was going through, Beth
began putting out long, tapered candles.

Rose's eyes widened. "Candles?" she cried as her
aunt lit first one, then the other. "You ordered candles? Since when are candles part of dinner?"

"There's dinner," Beth told her, raising, and lowering her delicately sculptured eyebrows mischie-
vously, "and then there's dinner."

And it was obvious that she was supposed to be
the main course.

"This is not going to happen," Rose protested.

Beth put the lighter into the deep recess of her
pocket.

"Dinner?" she asked innocently.

As if her aunt didn't know. "No," Rose insisted,
"what you're trying to achieve with dinner."

Her expression was suddenly completely without a
trace of guile as her aunt turned to look at her. Rose

could see how Beth had easily been regarded as a consummate actress in her time.

"Full stomachs and smiles, my dear," Beth told her. "That's my only goal." She looked at the minions she had summoned from her favorite restaurant, Claude's, and nodded, obviously well pleased. "Perfect."

Looking at the table as the servers backed away, melting into the background like dutiful fairy godmothers, Rose suddenly honed in on a glaring fact.

She looked accusingly at Beth. "Why are there only two places set?"

Beth's answer was simplicity itself. "Because only two people are eating."

It was bad enough when she'd thought this was for the three of them. A sinking feeling took over the pit of her stomach as she asked the question to which she already knew the answer, and hoped against hope that she was wrong. "*Which* two people?"

Beth looked no older than Rose as she replied, "Guess."

"Oh no." Beth shook her head adamantly. "I'm sorry, but no, I am not going to be left alone with him. I absolutely refuse."

Beth was apparently oblivious to the desperation behind Beth's words.

"It can't be helped, darling. I have a class to teach at the college."

Desperate, Rose looked for a way out. "Then I'll go with you. I've never heard you teach."

Beth waved a hand at the thought. "Long and boring. You wouldn't like it."

Rose had no intentions of giving up easily. "So I'll fall asleep. I could use the rest."

Beth looked at the table.

"No. You could use the nourishment. You're eating for two, you know." She slipped her arm around Rose's shoulders. "That's a very nice man in the other room, dear. He's not going to leap over the table and have his way with you." And then she stepped back and grinned wickedly as she glanced at Rose's trim figure. A figure that was going to expand very soon. "From where I stand, it looks like you've already both had your way with each other."

Rose remembered now how her father used to rant about how stubborn and headstrong his older sister was, not to mention unorthodox. Except that he'd called it flaky. For once, her father had understated a problem.

Rose felt a headache coming on. All over her body. "Aunt Beth, you're not helping."

Beth glanced at her watch.

"Why, my dear, I don't know what you mean. I just wanted you to have a nice dinner while I was gone. And now Matt is here to keep you company so you won't be alone." She was preparing to make her exit. An actress was nothing if she didn't know how to make entrances and exits. Even a retired one. "You could do a great deal worse than have a handsome male looking at you across the table. Believe me." She winked. "I know."

Her nerves were not up to this. Maybe Aunt Beth enjoyed these kinds of things, but she didn't. She wanted nothing more than peace and quiet. "I'm trying to put all that behind me."

Beth looked pointedly at Rose's flat stomach. "Some of it, I'm afraid, is ahead of you." She paused to brush a quick kiss across her niece's cheek and to squeeze her hand. "It's going to be all right, Rose. I promise."

Rose frowned. No, it wasn't. She knew that, had accepted it. Why couldn't Beth? "You're not in a position to make promises like that."

Beth shook her head. "Sometimes I swear you sound just like your father. Stop it," she chided playfully before she withdrew from the terrace.

She left Rose standing alone with Cornish game hen, sweet corn in wine sauce, mashed potatoes and a sinking feeling in her stomach. Pressing her lips together, she stared into the flickering flame of the candle closest to her, almost hypnotized.

Could wishes be made on candles that weren't sitting on top of a birthday cake?

If they could, she knew what she'd wish for. That she'd have a second chance at doing things differently. At doing them right. This time, she wouldn't get pregnant. That way, her affair with Matt could continue a little longer.

But that seemed to be capriciously out of her control. She wasn't supposed to have gotten pregnant. Heaven knew she'd taken precautions. She'd gone to her doctor and asked for birth control pills. He'd told her, as he'd written out the prescription, that even the best precautions were not one hundred percent foolproof.

That was her, all right, she thought cynically. A fool. A fool for loving a Carson when she was a Wainwright. A fool for skipping along the edge of a precipice in what was clearly delineated as earthquake country.

And now, she thought, her hand over her stomach, she'd slipped but good and the earthquake was imminent.

But not, she told herself, if she didn't say anything. It was up to her to prevent this major disaster. And telling her family who the baby's father was would be setting them all up for one hell of a disaster.

As would telling Matt that she was pregnant with his baby.

Which was why she needed him out of here as quickly as possible. That meant no romantic, candlelit dinners, no contact, no nothing. The longer he was here, the greater her risk of breaking down and telling him about the baby.

As much as she didn't want to marry Matt just to

give the baby a name, she knew that her heart would be irreparably broken if he didn't even make the offer. And there was no guarantee that he would. They'd never talked about marriage, never even hinted at it. It was a subject they'd both mutely agreed was closed to them. Theirs had been a purely, intensely physical relationship.

It was supposed to have been without strings.

But now a string threatened to hang them both.

"Wow."

Rose swung around, the sound of Matt's voice taking her heart prisoner.

But he was looking at the table, not her. Despite the situation, it made her smile. He'd always had a weakness for good food.

Stepping up to the table, he pulled out a chair and held it for Rose, waiting. She had no choice but to sit. "Your aunt always eats like this?"

It was a meal. One meal. How bad could it be? And she was hungry. Rose spread the napkin on her lap, avoiding looking at Matt. "Tonight she's not eating at all."

Beth had said as much to him, stopping by his room before she'd left. He continued to play dumb. "I noticed the two settings. Then it's just you and me?"

Her appetite suddenly fled. "You go ahead, I'm not hungry."

Fork already in hand, Matt put it down. "I'm not

about to eat all this by myself. I'm hungry, but I'm not a pig." He saw the grin slip over her lips. It warmed his heart to see it again. He'd forgotten just how much it could light up everything around her, including him. "What?"

She poured dressing on her salad, just to have something to do with her hands. "Just remembering the time you ate everything but the basket when we went on that picnic." She raised her eyes to his. "Your appetite was incredible."

His eyes skimmed over her. He hadn't known it was possible to miss someone so much in such a short period of time. "Yeah, I remember."

Rose felt a blush creeping up her neck, coloring her cheeks. "I was talking about the food."

"That, too."

For form sake, and because he was hungry, Matt tried to concentrate on the meal in front of him and to just make small talk. He was successful for about fifteen minutes, then, unable to avoid the question that had been nagging at him throughout the meal, he pushed aside his plate and surprised her by reaching for her hand.

"Why did you end it, Rose?"

Damn, and here she thought he wasn't going to bring anything up. She shrugged as she pulled away her hand. "I told you, it played itself out."

"No, it didn't." If that was what she was telling herself, then she was lying to both of them. "I can feel it still humming between us," he insisted. He reached for her hand again. "Chemistry."

She pulled her hand away at the last moment. The look in his eyes was so intense, it took effort not to look away. But she tried to make light of it.

"That's just the weather here. Lots of things hum in the air."

He didn't want to pretend anymore, but he couldn't tell her what he'd discovered was in his heart if she didn't feel the same way, if she kept denying that there was anything between them. "Can you honestly say you don't feel anything at all for me?"

I feel everything for you, but it doesn't change anything. She lifted her shoulders and let them drop carelessly.

"I feel friendship."

When she looked away, he took her chin in his hand and forced her to look at him again. "That's not what I'm talking about."

Her eyes narrowed and she dug in. "But that's what I'm talking about."

He stood, dragging her to her feet with him. "Kiss me."

That was the last thing in the world she wanted to do. Because she wanted to so much.

Rose tried to move away, but he held her hand fast. "Matt—"

His fingers curled around her, holding her hand to his chest. "Kiss me, and if you don't feel anything, then I'll go. A simple test, that's all.'' He searched her face, trying to see if he was making a complete idiot of himself, or if his gut instincts were right after all. ''That's all the condemned man asks, just a simple test.''

Panic sliced through her. If she kissed him, he'd know. ''The condemned man is supposed to get a last meal, not a last kiss.''

''We've bent a few rules before,'' he reminded her, thinking of the affair they'd been drawn into almost against their will. ''We can bend them again.''

''Matt—'' There was no getting away from it. Rose blew out a breath. She could do this, she told herself. She could pretend, just this once. She would kiss him as if she were kissing her brother. As long as she kept Justin's image fixed in her head, she could do this. Mentally, she crossed her fingers that she wasn't making a huge mistake. ''All right, just one kiss—and then you'll go?''

''If you don't feel anything,'' Matt qualified.

Taking another deep breath, Rose steeled herself. She offered her lips up to him as if she were bracing herself to kiss a frog.

Matt slipped his hands along her face, framing it with his powerful, sun-darkened fingers.

Praying, Rose told herself to breathe evenly as his mouth lowered to hers.

Justin, Justin, Justin, she struggled to remember.

It did no good.

Her heart started racing from the moment contact was made. Damn it, why couldn't she have more control over her own body? She was attempting to prevent World War Three back home—why couldn't she keep that foremost in her brain?

But it wasn't her brain that was the problem, it was the rest of her, and the rest of her had missed him something awful. Missed him even as she'd told him goodbye on the back steps of the library. The place had been her choice because it was nice, safe, neutral territory where she felt he couldn't suddenly vent his anger or, worse, sweep her into his arms and do exactly what he was doing right at this moment.

Melting her in the heat of his kiss.

Damn it, why couldn't she remember what Justin looked like? She was supposed to be thinking of her brother, not of what it had felt like to make love with Matt.

She had nothing to cling to, nothing to extinguish the fire that was springing up in her loins, nothing to cool the heat that was surrounding her, making her long for what had so recently been hers.

Matt had somehow pulled her into his arms when she wasn't looking and now it wasn't just their lips that were touching, but their bodies, too. She could feel his hard contours pressed against her soft, willing curves and all she could think of was the last time they had made love.

All she could long for was the next time.

But there wasn't going to be a next time. Ever. Why couldn't she remember that? Why was she betraying herself and everyone who mattered like this? She was supposed to be the strong one. Still waters ran deep and all that.

Still waters—nothing. She was sinking and sinking fast.

He wanted to take her, right here, right now, on this finely covered table amid the dishes of half-consumed chicken and untouched dessert. Rose was the only sustenance he needed or would ever need. He'd been hungry all these days without her and now he desperately wanted to fill himself with the taste, the smell, the touch of her.

She wanted him. Matt knew that, felt that. He had all the proof in the world right here in her lips, in the way her body leaned into his.

She wanted him.

But why was she trying so hard to deny this rare thing they had together? Why was she so bent on resisting him? And why had she run away?

It didn't make any sense to him.

The hell with sense, with decorum. They were alone together, beneath the stars, twenty stories above an improbably lush park in the heart of the busiest city in the country. He'd heard the front door close, knew that Beth Wainwright wouldn't be back for hours. She'd assured him of that.

They had time to make love. He had time to convince her that she belonged to him, and he to her.

Fear washed over Rose, chasing away some of the more erotic feelings skewering her. Fear had been summoned by those same erotic feelings. This couldn't go any further. She was going to lose it at any second and she knew it. Matt had always had this power over her, right from the very beginning.

Right from the first time he'd kissed her and stolen any inclination toward resistance she'd had.

Well, it couldn't happen again. She wouldn't allow it. She'd grown up a great deal in the last few months, especially the past six weeks. And now those consequences that had once been nebulous ghosts on the horizon had become a solid reality that threatened to come down and smother her.

Desperate to break free before it was too late, Rose wedged her hands against his chest. It took her a second to summon her breath, which had evaporated in the heat of the moment.

"All right," she declared, "I let you kiss me. Now will you go?"

Matt held her fast, unwilling to let her or the moment go. "You didn't 'let' me, Rose. You wanted me to kiss you."

She threw herself into the role of the contrary little witch and doubled her fists to beat on him. "You egotistical—"

Releasing her waist, he caught her by her wrists

before she made contact. His eyes stopped her far more effectively than his gesture.

"You wanted me to kiss you," he repeated, "almost as much as I wanted to kiss you. Why don't you just stop playing these games and come back with me to Mission Creek?"

With all her heart, she wanted nothing more.

Didn't he see how hopeless all this was? Even without the baby to complicate things. "So I can do what? Meet you in out-of-the-way places and steal a few minutes together?"

He didn't want things to change. They'd been so good. "What's wrong with that?"

With a sudden jerk, she pulled away her hands. "Everything. Look, that kiss proved nothing except that I'm physically attracted to you. I'm attracted to chocolate, too, but if I give in to it too much, I break out. So I keep consumption down to a minimum."

He tried to make sense out of what she was saying and came up short. "So you're telling me what? You want to see other men?"

She latched on to the excuse. Anything to keep him from taking her into his arms and kissing her again. Because this time she wasn't coming out again. "Yes, tons and tons of other men. Now will you go?"

He bought himself some time. "No."

"No?"

He sat again at the table, this time to cold chicken.

"I've still got a vacation to spend. And you're still my guide."

She stared at him in disbelief. "But I just told you—"

"I know what you told me and I respect that you want to see other men. I can understand that." Each word drove a knife through his heart, but he pretended otherwise. "There was no commitment to see each other exclusively," he reminded her.

He didn't love her, she realized with a piercing pain in her heart. It was his pride that was hurt, his pride that had made him follow her, nothing more. And since he now had proof that she was still attracted to him, that was all he wanted.

The big, dumb jerk.

To keep up the charade and keep from telling her what was in his heart, he started to eat the dessert, not even certain exactly what it was he was consuming.

"You know, you really should have some of this. It's delicious."

She fought the urge to take the pie and shove it in his face. "No thanks, I lost my appetite."

With that, she left the terrace. Before he could see her cry.

Five

Tired, Beth still paused to press her ear against the door of her apartment before putting the key into the lock.

Frowning, she remembered that it was a fire door and as such, she wouldn't be able to hear anything going on on the other side—if there was something going on on the other side.

She'd finished teaching her class hours ago. Rather than go home, she'd gone out for cappuccino with several of her students afterward. There'd been a time, she fondly recalled, when she would have stayed out until the wee hours of the morning, partaking of something a great deal stronger than coffee. But sadly, she mused, everyone had to make concessions to age, even she.

Once the students had started to drift away, saying something about having to get up early for class or work the next morning, she had opted to do a little romantic research and taken a ride around the park in one of the horse-drawn carriages.

It was just as lovely as she remembered it. The last

time she'd been on a carriage ride around the park, it had been with her last husband, Edward.

The best of the lot had been last, she'd mused, sentimentality getting the better of her. He'd been a keeper. Had he not died of a heart attack, she knew they'd still be married.

She could wish her niece nothing better than to have a love like the one she'd finally found with Edward.

Rose had it right under her nose, Beth thought. That Carson boy had a great deal of potential. She could tell just by looking at him. By what she saw in his eyes. It was true, they were windows to the soul.

She wasn't about to allow something as idiotic as an ancient feud ruin it for Rose, or him, either. She'd taken an instant liking to Matt. But that might have been because he reminded her a little of her last husband.

Beth sighed as she put her key into the lock. Turning it ever so slowly, she cracked the door open just a little.

Nothing.

Still exercising caution and discretion, Beth opened the door a little more until she could finally manage to slip through. Tiptoeing in, she looked around, hoping to see clothes strewn around, littering the floor all the way from the terrace to Rose's bedroom.

There was no litter, no clothes. Everything was as neat as she'd left it.

Battling disappointment, Beth marched out to the terrace and found that the candles had been blown out and only one of the plates looked as if it had been eaten from. The other had a salad that had obviously been toyed with, but never seriously entertained.

That would be Rose's, she concluded.

Beth sighed. Candlelight, moonlight and music and still nothing. This was going to be harder than she thought.

Crossing back into the living room, she closed the French doors leading to the terrace behind her. The people from Claude's would be by in the morning to clean up and take the dishes. She was far more concerned with the state of things within her apartment than what was left out on the terrace.

Were they up? Holed up in their separate rooms looking longingly at the wall that divided them? She could just envision them, too stubborn to make a move, sick with love for each other.

It was a scene worthy of a play. Maybe she'd tackle it someday. Right now, she had to tackle the protagonists of her would-be drama and make them see the light.

Beth caught her lower lip between her teeth, nibbling as she debated which of the two to talk to tonight. Or if she should exercise restraint and just let things go until morning.

Letting things go had never been her way, but she

wasn't entirely governed by her emotions. She knew the danger of pushing too much, too hard.

Her debate was abruptly aborted by the sound of a door being opened down the hallway.

The next moment she saw Matt's tall frame emerge from the shadows. He was carrying his suitcase in his hand.

It looked serious. Beth was beside him in an instant.

She gave him a long, studied look, her eyes resting on the suitcase. "I hope you're one of those eccentric people who likes to hold their possessions close to them when they go out for a walk."

Finding Beth in the living room had taken Matt by surprise. He didn't think anyone would still be up at this hour. But then, this was the city that never slept, he remembered. Obviously that went for some of its residents, too.

Because he wasn't familiar with all of her married names and didn't know which one she went by, he called her by the one he knew she'd once answered to. "I'm going back home, Miz Wainwright."

Not without my niece you're not, Beth thought.

She placed her hand over his on the suitcase, her intention clear.

"Give me the suitcase, boy." She saw the resistance in his eyes. "I don't want to wrestle you for it, but I will if I have to. And don't look at me like that.

I'm not some weird old woman. And I'm a lot stronger than I look.''

Matt laughed. ''I wasn't thinking of you as weird, or old,'' he added. He knew vanity when he saw it and although hers had a strange sort of endearing quality about it, he sensed her feelings could be hurt when it came to her age.

Beth smiled broadly at him, patting his cheek. *Such a dear boy.* ''I knew there was a reason I took to you so fast. Put the suitcase down, boy, and sit for a minute.''

He didn't like refusing her, but there was no point in his staying a minute longer. Rose wanted him gone and he wasn't about to beg her to reconsider. A man had his pride, after all.

''It's best if I go.''

She wasn't taking that as his final answer. ''You young people, you're all in such a hurry to go someplace and then when you get there, it's never what you thought you wanted. Stay awhile. Just give things a chance.''

He had given things a chance, had taken a chance and come out here to coax Rose back. If she'd had any true feelings for him, she wouldn't have needed much convincing. That kiss on the terrace would have been enough. It had been for him. But maybe Rose was right, maybe it was all strictly physical. People got over physical attraction in time.

''I was wrong to come here.''

She shook her head adamantly. "No, you're wrong to give up."

She sounded so convinced. Had Rose said anything to her? "What makes you so sure?"

Sitting on the sofa, she patted the place beside her. He had no choice but to take the seat—and hope she would say something to convince him.

"I'm old— Well, older at any rate," she corrected. "And I've been around the block more times than you've got fingers and toes, boy. Besides that, I've become a great judge of people. I wasn't watching the two of you for a whole minute before I got hit by the force of what's between you."

She was an actress and given to drama and exaggeration, he reminded himself, refusing to get his hopes up without some kind of real proof. There was no polite way to tell her, so he kept his peace.

"She told me it was over, Miz Wainwright."

"Beth," she corrected. "Calling me Miz Wainwright makes me think of my mother and I am *nothing* like my mother," she assured him.

Her mother was conservative and straitlaced. She'd stood beside one man all of her life and even as her mother took her dying breath, Beth had never been sure that she had loved her father, but she had stood by him, borne his children and his verbal abuse stoically. At her mother's deathbed, Beth had vowed that that kind of life would never be for her.

"Go on, I didn't mean to interrupt you." She smiled at him encouragingly.

He cited the evidence he'd gone over in his mind more than a dozen times tonight. "Rose said it was over. She said it here, she said it in Mission Creek. I've got no choice but to believe her."

Beth countered simply. "What did her eyes say?"

He stared at her, confused. He'd expected her to make an impassioned plea on the side of romance, not this. "Her eyes?"

"Yes, her eyes. A body can say whatever they want. Words are cheap, boy. You'll come to know that if you don't already. But what they feel is in their eyes—unless of course they're with the CIA, the way Clarence was."

The woman changed direction faster than a tennis ball in a championship match. "Clarence?"

The sigh that escaped Beth's lips was wistful and incredibly youthful. She was momentarily taken back to a time when she was not yet thirty, not yet seasoned in the ways of the world.

"Clarence Montgomery." She winked bawdily. "James Bond could have learned a thing or two from him. I know I did." She realized that she was going off on a tangent. "Sorry, didn't mean to get off the track. Where was I?"

"You were asking me if I had looked into Rose's eyes," he told her tactfully.

She beamed. "Oh, yes." She was looking up into his now. "Did you?"

Rose had eyes like wild violets in the field. They were absolutely mesmerizing. "That's where I got lost in the first place." His mouth curved in self-deprecating humor. "Funny thing is, I might never find my way back."

Beth patted his hand reassuringly. "You will, boy, but not if you go running off home."

They could go 'round and 'round about this all night, but it still wouldn't change things. "I wasn't running. I was being realistic."

She pinned him with a knowing look. "You were throwing in the towel."

Matt shrugged and looked away. "Maybe I just decided that I didn't need that vacation, after all."

The pressure of her hand over his caught his attention. "Maybe not, but you do need the woman. And she needs you." She lowered her voice. "More than you'll ever know."

Was Beth just spinning tales, or was this based on something, Matt asked himself. "Why? What did she say? Did she say something about me?"

He sounded positively eager. Beth was tempted, sorely tempted, to tell him everything. But that would be betraying a confidence and even for the best of reasons, she just couldn't let herself do that.

Besides, there were other avenues for her to try first. Like that lovely carriage ride around the park.

"I looked into her eyes," Beth told him, resting her case.

Eyes again. The woman was beginning to sound like a Gypsy fortune-teller, except that rather than using tea leaves or cards, she resorted to eyes. Nice gimmick, but he wasn't buying it.

"Well, I'm afraid I don't have that gift," he said, getting up.

She caught his hand so suddenly, she threw him off balance. With a quick yank, she pulled him onto the sofa.

"That's all right, Matt. I've got it for you. Stay," she urged in the face of his reluctance. "At least stay the night." Beth looked toward the pitch-black world just beyond her terrace doors. "This is no time to go running off in New York City. The place has been cleaned up, I grant you, but this isn't Mission Creek by a long shot. Don't go looking for trouble."

Especially if trouble was only a few feet away, Matt thought. In the room next to his.

Still, the woman had a point about leaving in the middle of the night. He didn't even have a plane reservation. He'd need to make that before he left. "Maybe you're right."

She was beaming again, delighted that he'd caught on so readily.

"Matthew, my boy, you'll discover soon enough

that I am *always* right. And when I'm not, I just make myself right.'' She winked, making him wonder if she was kidding or not. ''Now get to bed. I've got your itinerary ready for tomorrow and you're going to need your strength.''

He figured it was useless to repeat his plan to leave in the morning. He had an uneasy feeling Beth would confiscate his suitcase and his boots if he said that.

And maybe she was right. Maybe he was leaving too soon, giving up too quickly. Maybe he was running away at that. Running from something that he couldn't quite identify, but that scared the hell out of him because of its intensity.

Better to leave than to stick around. Relationships took too much trouble—had always been his motto. It wasn't anymore.

He nodded, temporarily surrendering. ''All right, I guess I can stay the night.''

Rising to her feet, she picked up the suitcase that was beside the sofa. ''And then some. Now go on, git,'' she said in her finest Texas accent, pointing down the hall to his room.

He laughed and kissed her cheek.

''Good night, Aunt Beth.'' Matt took the suitcase from her hand.

Yes, she thought as she watched Matt walk down the hall toward his room, it was going to be all right. She was going to see to it. Rose could be stubborn, but as Archy had once shouted at her while she was still living in the same house as he, there was no one under the sun more stubborn than she.

Rose woke up feeling more dead than alive.

She'd spent the better part of the night tossing and turning, unable to sleep because of the man who was only a few negligible feet away from her bed. A man she wanted, despite everything she'd said to the contrary, in her own bed.

And then when she'd finally managed to doze off in the wee hours of morning, a bout of nausea had overtaken her, sending her running to the bathroom to commune, headfirst, with the porcelain bowl while simultaneously praying that Matt wouldn't wake up and hear her or suddenly be struck with the need to make use of the facilities himself.

She swore this baby was sapping everything out of her, making her look pale and drawn. Or was the hopelessness she felt whenever she thought of her situation responsible for the way she looked lately?

Rose sighed. She was just too exhausted to sort all that out today. She didn't feel up to dealing with anything, least of all with seeing Matt.

The knock on her door set her teeth on edge as if long, sharp fingernails scraped across a chalkboard in her brain.

"Go away, I'm dead," she called, then pulled the pillow over her head, wishing her words were a prophesy. Could you die from misery?

From beneath her pillow, she heard the doorknob turn. She knew Beth meant well, but she couldn't deal with her exuberance, either. Not this morning. Peeking out from beneath her pillow, she began to beg off whatever it was that Beth had in mind.

Her words froze.

Matt—not Beth—was standing in her doorway.

The pillow fell to the floor as she scrambled into a sitting position, dragging her blanket to her as if the man standing there hadn't already seen her nude, in the afterglow of lovemaking.

Why couldn't he leave her alone and just let her die in peace?

Damn it, even with sleep lacing her lids and her hair all disarrayed, Rose was still the most beautiful woman Matt had ever seen. He felt himself becoming aroused just looking at her.

If he wasn't the kind of man he was, he would break out of the restraints he'd imposed upon himself and slip into bed with her this instant. He was certain he could erase the protest from her lips with next to no effort at all.

The taste of her mouth from last night was still on his lips, the imprint burned into his soul as well as his memory.

No, he thought again, next to no effort at all.

He smiled at her, remembering Beth's pep talk. "Morning."

Flustered, Rose blew out a breath. "Yes, it is. But

I would have figured that out without you.'' She gestured toward the light streaming into her room through the windows. ''Is there anything else earth-shattering you want to tell me?''

She was testy. He wasn't used to that. But he figured it was a hurdle he was going to have to overcome. Matt leaned against the doorjamb, his arms crossed at his broad chest. For now he was content to remain here, just looking at her and letting his thoughts drift.

But knowing it wasn't possible, he got down to business and answered her question. ''I was just wondering when we could get started.''

''Get started?'' she echoed dumbly. Just what the hell was he implying? What had Beth said to him? ''Doing what?''

He looked at her innocently. ''You're supposed to be my tour guide, remember? Your aunt went to the trouble to write up an itinerary for me.''

She scowled. Itinerary her foot. Beth was supposed to be on her side, not his.

''Are you still pretending you want to play tourist?'' She'd thought they'd gotten beyond that ruse last night. He wasn't interested in seeing the city; he was interested in reclaiming his pride, which she'd wounded by leaving him.

He grinned at her and she tried her best not to succumb.

''It's my story and I'm sticking to it.'' His eyes

locked with hers. Maybe Beth could read eyes, but he couldn't. When she wasn't being angry at him, he hadn't a clue what Rose was thinking. "This is supposed to be the most fascinating city in the country. So fascinate me."

"I'm not the city."

"But you know it better than I do," he pointed out. "You wouldn't want me to get lost, would you? Suppose I did and something happened to me. You'd never forgive yourself."

She sighed. This baby was absorbing all her tolerance, and right now whatever remained of it was being laid siege to by both Matt and her aunt. Being outnumbered didn't make her feel very friendly.

"Don't bet on it."

But that was exactly what he was doing. Betting on it. Betting the farm, the ranch and the whole nine yards. He took a step into the room and saw the guarded expression that came over her face.

"I could bring you breakfast. There's some fruit salad left over from last night."

Rose made a face. "Just apple juice." It was all she could hold down in the morning lately, and at times not even that.

"No coffee?"

The mere mention made the walls of her stomach pucker and twist.

"No, no coffee." She began to get out of bed, then

stopped. He was still standing there, watching her. "Do you mind? I have to get up and get ready."

"You didn't mind me watching you get dressed the last time," he reminded her, a hint of a wicked smile on his lips.

She remembered. Remembered slipping on her dress while wrapped in his warm gaze.

She struggled to keep back the thrust of desire before it could take hold.

"That was then, this is now." When he made no move to leave, Rose picked up a shoe and threw it in his direction. "Go."

"I'm going, I'm going." He laughed, ducking, as he left the room. The shoe landed against the closed door and fell to the floor.

Six

In the temporary housing of the Men's Grill, Spencer Harrison frowned as he flipped his cell phone closed. There'd been no answer. Again. This looked as if it was getting serious.

He liked to think that he wasn't given to needless worrying, although since entering his third decade and after becoming the local D.A., Spence had found himself doing a great many more worst-case scenarios than ever before. Including the period of time when he'd been a marine and he, Tyler, Ricky and Flynt had been held captive by the enemy.

Spence'd been the one who'd told the others to not give up hope, firmly believing that someone—most likely their commander, Phil Westin—would find them and help them fight their way out of the hellhole. And they had. Westin had engineered a plan that had freed them. An ex-juvenile delinquent earmarked for an early end, Spence had been miraculously plucked out of the destructive path his life had been headed and given another chance. Optimism had been his hallmark ever since.

Even so, experience had begun to slowly sink in,

tempering his optimistic bent. He'd known early on that life had a nasty habit of rising up and hitting you right between the eyes when you least expected it.

Hell, just look at what was happening with the commander. Westin had been sent to Central America on a secret mission to thwart a drug lord whose long tentacles were insidiously reaching more and more people in Texas. If anyone could bring down this El Jefe character, Spence knew it would be Westin.

Had he still been a marine, Westin's current status would have been M.I.A. No one knew where he was.

And now, on top of that, Spence couldn't reach Luke.

As far as he knew, none of the others had seen Luke for several weeks, either. Granted Luke Callaghan was the original millionaire playboy who owed no explanations to anyone. At thirty-four Luke could certainly take flight at a moment's notice if he wanted to, and he usually did.

But this time... Spence mused thoughtfully, studying the way the amber liquid coated the sides of his glass as he tilted it. This time it felt different. Luke could always be reached before, either by the pager built into his Rolex, or via the cell phone he was literally never without.

But Spence'd been unable to successfully reach Luke using either device.

Then an uneasiness had taken hold of him and began to eat away at him.

Spence knew for a fact that the celllular server Luke used, a high-tech, state-of-the-art service that was utilized by the government, didn't experience downtime or out-of-calling-range regions. So what was going on?

Where the hell was Luke?

A slight commotion at the entrance had Spence raising his eyes and looking in that direction. Just in time to see Tyler Murdoch and Flynt Carson walking in. He'd called each of them, asking them to meet him here.

"So here we are, back at the old watering hole," Flynt said, nodding a greeting at Spence as he took his seat.

Taking the chair on the other side of him, Tyler looked around.

From where he sat, the ex-demolitions expert looked a little uneasy. Curious, Flynt asked, "What is it?" as he looked at the man next to him.

Tyler would have never admitted this to another living soul, but he trusted Flynt and Spence beyond all reason. He'd trusted both with his life and if he were ever in any dire situation, he would have rested easier knowing that the man coming to his aid was either one of them, or Luke, Westin or even Ricky Mercado for that matter, despite the recent unpleasantness that had flared up between Ricky and the others.

"Ever since the bomb went off, I'm always a little

uneasy coming in here.'' He looked around at the temporary quarters. ''I keep expecting something else to blow up.''

Flynt dismissed the fear with a shrug of his shoulder. ''Bombs never strike twice in the same place.''

''That's lightning,'' Spence corrected him, ''and it does.''

Picking up the new menu, Tyler opened it. ''Well, that goes a long way in reassuring me.''

''It didn't have anything to do with you. It wasn't a random bombing,'' Flynt reminded him. ''We already found out that bomb was meant for Westin, to keep him from going to Central America on the mission. Sheriff Stone wanted to be sure that no one and nothing interfered with the sweet deal he and that band of henchmen of his had going with El Jefe, remember?''

Stone, along with the men who were part of a group known to one another as The Lion's Den, had since been arrested and were awaiting trial. At least one of El Jefe's tentacles had been lobbed off, but they all knew there were others. A great many others.

''Stone needn't have gone through all that trouble,'' Tyler observed cynically, ''seeing as how someone's obviously gotten to Westin down there.''

He tried not to worry about his former commander, but it wasn't easy. There were regions in Central America where a man could get lost and never be heard from again.

Trying not to dwell on what he couldn't do anything about, he turned to look at the honey-blond waitress who had approached their table. Just for a second, there was something vaguely familiar about the young woman, but he dismissed it.

"Scotch," he ordered, then turned back to the group. "I take it Westin hasn't surfaced yet?"

Spence shook his head. "He's still missing." He waited while Flynt ordered a drink and asked for a refill. "Speaking of missing, have either of you heard anything from Luke?"

"Why?" Tyler asked. "You think he's the father?"

The question came out of left field. Spence finished his drink, setting the chunky glass down just as the waitress returned with their orders. "Of who?"

"The baby Flynt found. Lena. Boy, I thought D.A.'s were supposed to be sharp," Tyler quipped. "They must have really lowered the standards with you." His smile faded a little as he looked at Spence more closely. "What's the matter, Harrison, you look as if you've got the weight of the world on your shoulders." Suspicion gave way to uneasiness. It wasn't like Spence to look so solemn. "Why did you ask us to meet you here today, anyway?"

Taking his glass from the waitress, Spence nodded his thanks and took a long sip before answering. He wanted to dull the edge of his concern, just for the moment.

"To look at your ugly mugs," he retorted, and then he added more soberly, "and to ask if Luke's been in touch with either of you."

"Not me," Flynt testified, taking a long sip of his own drink.

"Me, either," Tyler added. "I doubt he's talked to Ricky, either."

They all knew that the fifth member of their group, the group that had gone through both the Virginia Military Institute and the Gulf War together, was estranged from them.

Ricky Mercado's family had ties to the Texas Mafia via his uncle, who was head of one of the mob families, and his own father, Johnny, who was an unwilling participant, blackmailed into remaining with the mob to protect his family and keep them out of harm's way. Johnny's efforts were largely unsuccessful. His wife had been eliminated by the mob as a warning. His son Ricky had apparently succumbed to the lure of the mob, forsaking his former friends because of an argument that had ensued over the death of his sister, Haley, who had drowned while in the company of Luke, Spence, Flynt and Tyler. She had fallen overboard while the four had been intoxicated. They hadn't even realized she was gone until it was too late. Ricky never forgave his former comrades-in-arms.

Tyler leaned forward, looking at Spence. "You worried about Luke?"

"A lot could happen to a man out there," Spence said, defending his concern. "Look at Westin."

It was obvious that they were all trying to maintain positive thoughts about the commander's situation. "Hey," Flynt retorted, "despite the fact that the man is richer than God, Callaghan can take care of himself, remember?"

"That's what we all said about Westin, too," Spence reminded them.

He took out his cell phone again.

Haley Mercado aka Daisy Parker, Lone Star Country Club waitress, felt her heartbeat as she heard the three men mention her brother Ricky when she served them drinks. They were the same men who had been brought up on negligent homicide charges involving her so-called accidental "death." She'd only learned of the charges after the fact. By then, she had been in London and had already undergone plastic surgery.

Staying dead, the circumstances of which she had purposely staged herself, was the only way she had of ensuring that she would remain alive. She'd later discovered that Judge Carl Bridges had arranged for her escape, and had gotten the four men acquitted of all charges.

It was the judge who had told her about her mother and who had arranged to sneak her into her mother's hospital room disguised as a nun. It had been the last meeting between mother and daughter. Haley's mother had passed away that evening. The official diagnosis differed with the truth.

Isadora Mercado had been smothered.

The four men at the table hadn't mentioned Ricky again. They were now talking about Luke. He was missing, according to Spence.

Fear gripped her heart.

She hurried away, afraid that one of them might suddenly recognize her, despite the great lengths she had gone to with her disguise. A small part of her felt empowered, to move among them this way without their knowing who she was. But linked to that was fear that one or the other might suddenly look into her eyes and see the young girl they used to know, the tag-along who had been more than half in love with Luke.

The woman they had almost gone to prison over.

Damn, but she looked good enough to eat.

Matt Carson smiled to himself.

That was the very same thought he'd had about Rose when he'd first walked into the library that day, looking for an old magazine article about horse ranching someone had recommended to him.

Rose had been behind the centrally placed information desk. When he'd approached feeling very lost, she'd primly asked if she could be of any service.

He'd kept to himself the answer that had instantly

popped up in his mind. She hadn't looked the type to indulge in risqué repartee. Instead he'd asked her if he could take anything out of the library he wanted. When she'd said yes, he'd asked if he could take her out.

She'd almost shown him the door, until he'd back-tracked and told her about the article. She'd pointed him toward the computer. Faced with trying to use a device he'd religiously steered clear of, Matt had thrown himself on her mercy and asked for help. She'd had no choice but to give it.

By the time the article had been located and printed, Matt had been completely captivated by her smile, the supple body that moved so sweetly beneath the light-blue dress she'd been wearing, and the scent of jasmine that lingered around her like a seductive cloud, making him almost feel giddy.

He'd asked her out before ever knowing her name, or she his.

Discovering she was a Wainwright had momentarily taken him aback, but hadn't deterred him. After all, what he'd had in mind was to be something strictly casual, a good time for both, nothing more.

Apparently, discovering that he was Ford Carson's son had been a definite stumbling block for Rose. She turned down his invitation to dinner, and continued to turn him down each time he'd asked her out, though secretly taken, she later told him, with his de-termination. Matt began visiting the library on a regular basis, to "browse" and to apply himself to breaking down her defenses.

Because Rose resisted him—something no other woman he'd encountered had ever done—Matt had been completely determined to wear her down.

Waging a never-ending campaign that lasted for several months had turned out to be worth it.

God, he thought now, was it ever worth it.

The first time he'd kissed her, it was to wipe a trickle of vanilla ice cream from the corner of her mouth. That was the excuse he'd given her and his own heart had raced like a young schoolboy's a moment before his lips met hers.

She'd tasted like heaven and he'd been completely hooked.

It wasn't long after that that they'd made love for the first time, he recalled, remembering everything about the sun-drenched afternoon in the open field. He'd gotten hooked on that, too. Alarmingly so, he now realized.

Right from the start, he just couldn't seem to get enough of her, but he'd consoled himself with the fact that this, as everything else, would lose its luster for him. It always had before, though he'd never experienced anything so intense. After all, Rose represented a conquest and when they'd made love, that meant she'd been conquered.

But something had happened to him during his campaign to set siege to her and storm her ramparts.

Matt had become so entrenched, so caught up in trying to win all the game pieces, that he'd lost his way back to his side of the board.

He'd completely lost himself.

He wanted to find himself again, to find the man who had loved his freedom more than anything else in the world. The trouble was, he'd ceased to remember what that man looked like.

Freedom, he was beginning to suspect, was just another term for rootlessness. And a part of him was getting tired of being rootless.

Matt got up from the dining room table where he'd been taking coffee with a sleepy-eyed Beth, his conversation with the woman halting in midword when Rose emerged from her bedroom.

He'd never seen Rose wear anything like this back home. She had on a short, wraparound skirt that showed her legs off to their full advantage and a cropped electric-blue blouse that barely covered her midsection.

The woman was making his mouth water.

Matt put his half-empty cup down as an afterthought. ''You ready?''

Beth seemed to come to life just then. ''Oh, but you can't leave without having breakfast, dear.'' The protest was directed toward Rose. Ada, Beth's part-time housekeeper, was busy in the kitchen, so Beth leaned across the table to peer into the next room. ''Ada, Rose'll have the eggs.''

The mention of food, any food, sounded gross. Rose pressed her lips together, sternly telling her stomach to stop lurching.

"Only if you want to see me juggle them." Rose did her best to sound cheerful instead of ominously nauseated.

But Beth insisted, "Breakfast is the most important meal of the day."

What was Beth doing? Rose thought in horror. Her aunt knew about her morning sickness.

"I never eat breakfast," Rose told her adamantly. "It slows me down."

"Can't have that," Matt agreed.

He wanted Rose in the best frame of mind today. Day One of his plan to win her back. Matt took Rose's hand, but she twisted her fingers out of them.

"I'll be your guide, Matt," she said, "but we need to set a few ground rules. Ground Rule Number One—no touching."

After talking to Beth last night, he'd made up his mind that he was going to have to be extremely patient. "What if the bus is crowded?"

"We'll be taking cabs. You'll sit on your side, I'll sit on mine." Rose heard him sigh and raised her eyes to his face. "It's the only way."

Matt nodded his head, appearing resigned to the edict, convinced in his heart that he could make her forget about it quickly enough. The woman who'd kissed him on the terrace last night was not going to be able to indefinitely maintain the barriers that were being reconstructed this morning.

"If that's the way it's gotta be, that's the way it's gotta be."

Matt turned to retrieve his Stetson from the coffee table in the living room where he'd left it last night, and caught Beth's eye. He winked at her, and Beth smiled conspiratorially.

They were cooking up something, Rose thought. Well, two could play at this game. And she had more at stake than he did because she was playing for two.

Picking up her purse from the hall table, she looked at Matt. "Where do you want to go first?"

Busy studying the curve of her legs, he was temporarily brought up short.

"I suggested you take him to the top of the Empire State Building," Beth interjected. "It's a fantastic view and that's where King Kong took Fay Wray."

"On their last outing together, if I remember correctly," Rose interjected. "They broke up right after that."

Matt vaguely remembered seeing the original version as a little boy. He looked from one woman to the other. "I'm a little slow here. Am I being called a beast?"

Rose could feel a smile struggling to gain space on her lips, despite her resolve to remain aloof and distant. "I never said a word."

Wedging herself between them, Beth threaded an

arm through each of theirs as she escorted them to the front door.

"And after that," she continued, "you could go to an art museum. It's an exciting way to spend the afternoon," she told Matt, "looking at all those paintings by artists who opted to live out their dreams through their choice of paint, putting their passion into their work." She looked at Rose pointedly.

Rose met her head-on. "Are you trying to tell me something, Aunt Beth?"

Beth's face became a testimony to sheer innocence. "Only to enjoy every moment of life that you can. You'll never have this minute again."

Rose slanted her eyes toward Matt. "There's something to be said for that."

"If you're trying to hurt my feelings, I've got a tough hide." Now that his mind was made up, she would have to do a lot better than that to make him back off and go home.

The comment broadened the playing field for the smile Rose was having no success at blocking. As she remembered it, his hide wasn't all that tough. It was hard, and strong, with contoured muscles he'd earned while putting in twelve-hour days in the saddle, but it definitely wasn't tough. Not to the touch.

Abruptly, she stopped and upbraided herself for letting her mind wander.

"Have fun, you two," Beth said, all but pushing them out the door.

"Penny for your thoughts," he whispered against Rose's ear as they walked out.

His breath wound its way into her senses as it caressed the delicate skin along her neck.

It was best all around if he hadn't a clue as to what she was thinking, Rose thought. Actually, it was best if she wasn't thinking at all.

They got into the elevator and as Matt reached out to push the button for the ground floor, his hand brushed her breast. Rose backed away as if he'd burned her.

"Sorry," he mumbled, looking as if it had been a genuine accident on his part rather than anything he might have calculated.

She shrugged as if it was okay. But it wasn't.

It was hard not to remember everything she had felt for Matt while standing beside him in a small box swiftly making its way down twenty floors to the lobby.

Especially since she was still feeling it.

Seven

The moment they stepped onto the street, they were engulfed in a sea of people.

It wasn't difficult for Matt to imagine how a person could very easily be swept away. Scanning both sides of the street, he noted hordes of cars cluttering the roads and packs of people on corners either waiting for the lights to change or pushing their way across to the other side, fighting both pedestrians and vehicles trying to make turns.

He'd never seen so much life stuffed into such a small area—and that included corrals at branding time.

Because he was unaccustomed to the noise level, Matt leaned his head in closer to Rose.

"How many people did you say this city has?"

She shifted slightly, not wanting to be distracted by his breath along her skin. She was aware enough of him as it was.

"I didn't," she pointed out. She looked around, debating her first step. "About eight million, I think."

"Are they all out on the street right now?"

Last night when his plane had finally landed at

JFK, he'd been focused on finding Beth's apartment and had noticed very little of anything else. He'd made his way out of the terminal to find a fleet of cabs waiting for his selection and ultimate direction. Taking the first vehicle at the curb, Matt had given the driver Beth's address, which he'd obtained through no small pains, and been dropped off at her apartment building.

There could have been a flock of penguins dressed in eighteenth-century regalia standing in the lobby and he probably wouldn't have noticed them. Rehearsing what he'd say and trying to keep his feelings under wraps had left little space in his brain for noticing anything.

Now, however, the amount of teeming humanity that crowded the streets of New York at any one time was beginning to sink in.

"No," Rose answered, straight-faced. "They're not all out now."

And then she laughed, remembering her own first reaction to the city. Ten years old, she'd been dumbstruck by the wonder of it all. It had been summer then, too. But somehow the mugginess of it hadn't registered. It was the summer that Aunt Beth had returned to Mission Creek for a visit.

Before she'd left, she'd offered to take one of them to New York with her for a month. Susan had been too young and Justin had had no interest in the city.

She'd been the only one who'd been curious enough to volunteer.

It had been like a trip into wonderland. Beth had taken her to the theater, to the museums and the Village, ensuring she experienced all the culture that New York had to offer. She smiled at the memory.

"What?" Matt liked to watch the way her smile claimed all of her, like sunshine creeping over the darkened land at daybreak.

"I'm just remembering my first time here. There were so many different languages, so many different-looking people, I thought I'd been dropped in the middle of a foreign country. I guess it can be pretty overwhelming," she agreed.

That's putting it mildly, he thought. His eyes narrowed as Matt looked in the distance. The block was sloped just enough for him to note a huge cluster of people shoving slowly forward along the sidewalk. "Is there some kind of parade today?"

She had no idea what he was talking about. "Not in the middle of July."

"Then what's that?" He pointed toward the sidewalk crowd several streets away.

Rose could barely make out the subway entrance at the end of the block. "Just people going to work."

"Oh." It looked like the beginning of some kind of mass movement to him, but she knew better. "If you say so."

Turning to look at the building they'd just exited, Matt took in the adjacent skyscrapers.

He shook his head. The only kind of skyscrapers he liked were mountain ranges. "Kind of dwarfs a man," he muttered.

Rose looked up at the building and then at him. One side of her mouth curved slightly. "I'd imagine it takes more than a few buildings to dwarf you."

Her comment, offered so casually, surprised him. He could feel a warmth spreading slowly within his chest. Maybe coming here hadn't been a fool's errand, after all. Maybe Beth was right, there was hope.

"Thanks."

Rose shrugged, realizing her error too late. She had to be careful or he'd figure out that she was only pretending to not care about him. "Just calling it the way it is."

If she felt that way, he didn't understand her behavior. "Then why—"

Way ahead of him, Rose put her finger to his lips before he could say anything further.

"Rule Number Two," she announced. "The only way this is going to work is if we don't talk about certain things. Like the recent past." Realizing she was far too close to his lips for her own comfort, Rose let her finger slip down. "Let's just enjoy the day, all right?"

Damn, did she know how much control he was exhibiting by not just sweeping her into his arms and kissing her hard, right here, until they were both senseless? But somehow, he managed to keep up the charade.

"All right, but you just broke Rule Number One." When she looked at him quizzically, Matt elaborated. "No touching, remember?"

She knew she was only encouraging him, but she couldn't seem to hold the amused smile back from her lips. "That rule was for you, not me."

"Oh." He pretended to think it over for a moment. "Doesn't seem very fair."

"No," she said more to herself than to him. "Lots of things aren't."

But she couldn't dwell on that, couldn't dwell on the unfairness that separated her from him, that would ultimately separate their baby from him. With a surge of determination, she roused herself.

"All right, Aunt Beth said we should start with the Empire State Building. Let's get a cab. Although..." Her voice trailed off as she looked out on the street and saw myriad cars, all moving slowly, all honking. There were more than a smattering of cabs sprinkled through the mix. They weren't moving any faster than the rest of the traffic. "We might make better time if we just walk."

Gauging the speed of the vehicles, Matt mused silently, they could probably make better time shuffling all the way. He hooked his arm through hers.

"Sounds like a plan to me."

Her first instinct was to leave her arm just exactly where it was, pressed against his side as they began to weave their way through the sea of humanity. But self-preservation dictated that she had to disentangle herself if she was to maintain a shred of the boundaries she was trying to impose on both of them.

"Rule One," she reminded Matt as she slipped her arm out.

He inclined his head, telling himself to be patient. Patience won a man everything.

"Rule Number One," he murmured, letting his hand drop to his side.

Relieved, Rose flashed him a smile as she took the lead.

"Hell of a view," Matt was forced to agree. They were standing on the outdoor observation deck on the eighty-fifth floor of the Empire State Building. He'd expected that there would be a breeze, relief from the insufferable heat that was plaguing the city, but the humidity was just as intense here as anywhere else. "If you like looking at other buildings."

"It's even better if you look through one of these," Rose said, pointing to one of the many silver telescopes placed equidistantly along the deck. "For a dollar you can get a close-up of a breathtaking view."

"I'm looking at one now, and I didn't even have to pay anything."

He had the prettiest tongue when he wanted to.

Rose could feel a blush bubbling within her veins a split second before it began to slowly slip over her.

She had to be a prize idiot, she thought, blushing at a compliment from Matt Carson. The man had seen her nude, for heaven's sake. Why was she blushing like some silly adolescent schoolgirl looking up at her very first crush?

But this was a new twist for him. Matt had never been that complimentary before, she recalled.

She kept her face forward, wishing there was some sort of cool breeze stirring instead of these waves of heat that were assaulting her.

"Has Aunt Beth been coaching you?" she asked nonchalantly.

He shook his head as if he and Beth hadn't had a little heart-to-heart close to midnight last night. "Only about where we should go in the city. Why?"

She lifted a single shoulder. "No reason. That just didn't sound like anything you'd say on your own, that's all."

The hot wind stirred a few tendrils loose about her face. He lightly tucked in one strand, then, at her raised brow, backed away. He wondered how much longer he was going to have to endure this penance.

"Maybe I've learned a few things since you walked out on me."

She hated the way that sounded, hated the way that made her seem. It was supposed to have been a mutual dissolution. "I didn't walk out on you."

"Okay," he said agreeably. "Run out, then." Which, in his opinion, was more like the truth. She'd run out, all right. Run out wearing high heels that she'd figuratively used to stomp all over his heart.

She shifted over to a scant bit of shade from an overhang.

"I didn't do that, either," she insisted firmly. "It was a mutual agreement."

She had been very careful to make it seem as if he'd wanted it to be over, too, although she suspected in his case wounded pride had prompted it.

That was a load of horse manure, Matt thought, and she knew it. "For it to be mutual, both of us had to be of like mind. As I recall—"

She looked at him sharply. "Rule Number Two."

Matt sighed. He was going to have to work at holding on to his temper. There wasn't anything to be gained by forcing the issue. Not yet.

"Right."

Walking by her, he approached a telescope and dug into his pocket, looking for a dollar's worth of change. He dropped the coins in the slot. A clink announced that the shield from the viewfinder had been lifted. Bending over, he looked through it.

"There's a pigeon walking around on the roof down there," he observed, then glanced up at Rose. She'd moved closer to him, he noticed. "Hardly seems worth it, paying a dollar to see a pigeon when

I could see them wandering through the garbage on the street for free.''

She inclined her head, as if seeing the merit in his argument. ''But this is a pigeon as seen from the observation deck of the Empire State Building.'' A smile entered her eyes as she regarded him. There were parts of him that were so like a boy, she thought. ''It's all in your perspective.''

His eyes held hers for a moment. ''Yes, I guess it is.''

Flustered, Rose stubbornly attributed the feeling more to a hormonal imbalance than what Matt was saying to her.

Or the way he was looking at her.

That, and the heat, which was becoming utterly unbearable. Though she knew it was useless, she began to fan herself with the information booklet Matt had picked up.

The light clothes she had on were sticking to her as if she'd bathed in honey. The sun was beating down unmercifully and at this height, it felt as if it was waging a personal vendetta against her. She looked at Matt.

''Maybe we'd better find something a little cooler to do.''

''Not possible,'' he replied, backing away from the telescope. He looked down at her face. ''Not while I'm anywhere near you.''

Damn, why did he have to say such nice things? It

was hard enough not to want him when he kept his mouth shut, but when he talked like that....

"Matt—"

He raised a brow. "Going to make up a new rule? Because I didn't break one or two. I didn't touch you and I didn't say anything about you leaving me."

The look in his eyes raked across her heart. "Maybe this was a bad idea." Turning on her heel, she began to march toward the exit and the elevators just beyond.

Moving quickly, Matt managed to get in front of her. He raised his hands as he did so.

"Look, Ma, no hands." And then he sobered just a little. "Sorry, Rose, I'll behave." He looked at her soulfully. "I promise."

Rose sighed, knowing she was crazy for doing this. But she couldn't seem to help herself, not where Matt was concerned. He'd be gone again soon enough, she thought. One way or another.

"All right," she conceded. "Let's go see St. Patrick's Cathedral." He'd have to be on his best behavior there, she reasoned.

Because of near-traffic gridlock and the fact that she didn't relish the thought of going underground to the subways on a day like today, they walked from the Empire State Building on 34th Street to St. Patrick's Cathedral on Fifth Avenue and 50th Street.

Ordinarily, it wouldn't have been that much of a

walk for Rose. She'd done it lots of times handily. But she'd never been in the early stages of pregnancy before, and the merciless heat was working against her. It had rained a little in the middle of the night and rather than offer relief, it had added to the oppressive atmosphere, creating more humidity.

It was getting harder and harder for her to concentrate or even to place one foot in front of the other. Rose felt as if she'd walked into a fog.

On the way to the cathedral, she'd used the excuse of window-shopping to stop and subtly catch her breath, hoping that her heart would stop beating like a lost hummingbird searching for a perch.

By the time they arrived at the cathedral, she could have wept. It felt as if she'd reached sanctuary. The elegant edifice embraced her with its coolness, thanks to a powerful air-conditioning system. As she moved slowly through the main portion with its side altars, stained-glass and celebrated statues, she silently thanked God for the opportunity to regain her bearings.

Being inside the majestic church touched off a sadness within her. There'd been a time when she'd dreamed about getting married, about a big church wedding with all the trimmings. But time had slipped by and there had been no one who moved her heart.

Until Matt.

She glanced at him covertly as he stood in front of one of the side altars, reading the description of the saint portrayed there. And now that she'd lost her heart, she was still no closer to that huge church wedding than she was years ago when she'd only fantasized about it.

Eventually, it was time to leave. Refreshed though she felt, the moment they stepped outside, the hot air assaulted Rose like a fireball that had been lobbed directly at her. As if in a trance, she clutched the banister and slowly made her way down the steps until she reached the street.

She felt as if she'd been through a wringer. The air was almost tangible and she felt its weight on every inch of her body. Reaching blindly, she grabbed Matt's arm, afraid that her knees were going to buckle.

"Breaking Rule Number One? Oh, I forgot. You can't break it, only I can." When he looked at her, his joking tone evaporated the way the hot moisture in the air refused to. "Rose, are you all right?" Her cheeks were so flushed, she looked as if she'd liberally smeared blush on them.

She could make out his voice, but it was echoing in her brain.

"I'm…fine. Maybe…we should go somewhere for…something cold to…drink."

The words dribbled from her lips as she struggled to keep the world in focus, but it insisted on winking in and out like a light show.

The next moment the lights disappeared, as did the bones in her legs.

"Rose!"

Lunging, Matt caught her just as her body went limp. Scooping her into his arms, his heart pounding, he was momentarily lost as to his next move. Did he take her to the hospital? Bend with her right here and lay her on the sidewalk until she came to?

And then someone placed a hand gently on his arm.

Jerking around to look behind him, he saw an older, petite woman dressed in a summery blue skirt, blue vest and white blouse. She was wearing a short blue veil that hid part of her hair, but allowed a shock of white to peer out. She looked at him solicitously with bright, intelligent blue eyes.

"Is she all right?"

"I don't know," Matt replied. "She just suddenly passed out."

"Perhaps it's the heat. Why don't you bring her inside for a moment?" the woman coaxed. "I'm Sister Mary Katherine. I'm sure Father Malkowski won't mind if you bring her into the office to rest a bit."

Turning, the nun led the way back up the stairs. Matt followed, surprised at how many people had just continued on their way, shifting curious glances at him but not stopping. He was grateful that the nun had come along when she had.

Sister Mary Katherine led him to a small office. There was a well-worn desk in the room, shelves stuffed with books lining two of the walls and a creased burgundy leather sofa in the corner against a third. The sofa faced the desk and a large window that looked into a side yard.

"Place her there," the nun urged.

As he made to comply, Sister Mary Katherine stepped into what turned out to be a tiny bathroom. Matt could hear water running. He brushed Rose's hair from her forehead and took her hand. Her eyes were still shut. Nervous, he felt for a pulse.

"Was she feeling ill?" the nun asked, coming back into the room.

"Not that she mentioned." Feeling completely inept, he rubbed Rose's hands. Her face continued to look flushed.

Leaning over Rose, Sister Mary Katherine placed a cold, wet cloth on her forehead. "Is she by any chance pregnant?"

"No," Matt responded immediately. And then he paused. The thought had never occurred to him. "That is… No," he concluded again.

Rose would have told him if she were pregnant.

Wouldn't she?

Unsure, he looked down at the woman he had involuntarily lost his heart to. The woman who had turned his world completely upside down while never asking him for a thing.

The nun beside him was nodding. "Then it's probably this ungodly weather—you'll pardon the pun," she added with a twinkle in her eye. "That's one of the reasons we keep so many smelling salts on hand." She indicated the small capsule she was holding in her palm. "More than one light-headed visitor has found herself suddenly communing with the floor."

She laid a hand on Matt's shoulder. "I'm sure your young lady will be just fine. Hold her still now. We don't want her falling off the sofa and adding to her troubles." Waiting until Matt placed his hands on Rose's shoulders, Sister Mary Katherine broke open the capsule beneath Rose's nose.

An acrid smell immediately assaulted her nose. Rose twisted and turned, trying to get away from the pungent odor. A small moan escaped her lips. She jerked suddenly and would have bolted upright if someone hadn't been restraining her.

Rose's eyes were watery as she blinked, trying to focus on her surroundings. The last thing she remembered was standing outside of St. Patrick's, trying to get the world to stand still.

"What…what happened?"

Relief washed over him. For now, Matt packed away the sister's innocent question. The idea was absurd, but it nagged at him anyway. Still, it would keep.

"You fainted."

She'd never fainted before in her life. That was for weaklings, not her. "No, I didn't," Rose protested incredulously.

"Gave your young man here quite a scare," Sister Mary Katherine told her.

Stunned, she stared at Matt. "You brought me back into the church?"

"Coolest place there is right now," the nun told her. "I'm Sister Mary Katherine and you're welcome to remain here as long as you like. Or I could hail a cab for you if there's somewhere you'd rather go."

"No, that won't be necessary. I'm fine," Rose assured her, trying to sit up. The only problem was, Matt was still holding her in place. "Matt, let go of my shoulders. I'm fine."

He pulled back his hands. "Right. Rule One."

She heard the slightly bitter edge to his tone. "No, not Rule Number One. Just a request." She bit her lower lip, still feeling woozy. "I really fainted?"

"Dropped like a stone." He saw her glance down at herself. Probably looking for any bruises that might be beginning to form. "I caught you before you had a chance to hit the ground."

She looked at him ruefully. "I guess I should thank you for breaking a rule."

The flush was receding from her cheeks. She was starting to look like her normal self. "Only if you want to."

Sister Mary Katherine folded her hands in front of herself, glad that she wasn't needed any longer. "Well, if you young people will please excuse me, I do have errands to run."

"We'll be on our way," Rose told her, rising. Her legs felt a little wobbly as she stood, but at least they held her. "And thank you."

Sister Mary Katherine squeezed her hand. "Don't thank me, thank your young man, my dear. He's the one who caught you."

Yes, Rose thought, looking at Matt. He certainly did.

Eight

The inordinately good-looking young man standing in front of Beth Wainwright was pouring out his heart in a Marlon Brandoesque voice that sublimated his own, richer tones.

Tucker Stephens was one of eighteen young, would-be thespians who comprised her intermediate acting class and gathered around her twice a week for three hours to absorb her direction and expertise. Tonight they were gathered in her living room and the hour was getting late.

In spite of the fact that Tucker's performance was rather good, aside from the somewhat grating accent he had affected, Beth was having trouble concentrating. Her mind was elsewhere.

A week had passed.

A week in which, she knew, Matt continued to play the part of the patient, curious tourist and Rose continued to play his polite but distant guide. Beth knew this was the way things were going because Matt had filled her in. Beth also knew that Rose's young man was beginning to think about giving up again. He wasn't the caveman type, he wasn't about to grab

Rose by the hair and drag her to his lair, to keep her there until she came to her senses.

That alone recommended Matt to her, Beth thought. There just had to be some way to cut to the chase, to get Rose to see past her stiff, noble sentiments and cleave to the man who would make her life that much more worthwhile if she just allowed him.

In her heart, Beth knew that Matt was the one for Rose and she was positive that Rose knew it, too.

If only that damned stubborn Wainwright streak wasn't there...

Rose needed, Beth suddenly decided as Tucker called out to an imaginary wife his character had wronged, a catalyst. Something to set things in motion and to send Rose into Matt's arms.

Or someone...

A thought came to her, taking root swiftly.

Beth began to smile.

Tucker ended his scene to a smattering of applause from the rest of the students.

They were a hard lot to share praise, she thought. Already competitors.

"Very good, Tucker," Beth said, rising from her winged chair from where she held court over the class.

"Well, that's all for tonight's class." They began to gather their things together. "I want you all to rehearse those scenes we selected earlier this evening and be ready to go on the next time we meet.'' Like a queen sending her soldiers to the wars, Beth waved them off to the front door. All except for Bryce Keaton.

Bryce had been her prize student more than a year ago. She had even recommended him to an old friend of hers who'd been producing an off-Broadway play at the time. Graduated now, Bryce still sat in on her classes, saying he never stopped learning from her.

They had an affinity for each other that both enjoyed. ''Oh, Bryce.'' She turned toward him as the last of the students filed out. ''Would you mind staying a moment longer? I'd like to discuss something with you.''

Beth saw one of the students nudge another as they left and didn't have to guess what they were probably thinking. She smiled to herself. She had always liked being the center of attention, the mystery woman people were always guessing about. Bryce had taken a break between graduating high school and going on to college. He'd allowed himself a few years to bum around Europe and earn his own way around the world before enrolling in college. Hence, he was older than the others and seemed years older than that.

She, on the other hand, never thought of herself as any older than twenty-nine.

Bryce smiled at her as she closed the door. ''So, what's on your mind?'' he asked. ''I could see those wheels up there suddenly turning when Tucker was on. Want me to give him some help nailing down his motivation?''

She waved her hand at that. ''Very kind of you, dear. But, no.'' She smiled at him. ''He's no Bryce, but then, neither were you when you first came to my class.''

As she spoke, she slowly circled Bryce, looking at him from all angles as if she'd never seen him before. He'd come to class dressed completely in black, which had given her the idea in the first place. The more she thought about it, the more she liked it.

He certainly had the body for it, she silently approved. Still, she had to ask. ''I think I remember you saying you were into track and field when you were in college.''

''Yes, I was.''

She stopped in front of him. He was a good deal taller than she was. ''How fast can you run?''

''Why? Are you planning to chase me?''

He almost sounded as if he drawled when he said that. The way that Matt did. It made her feel a little homesick. She smiled. ''Maybe later. What's your best time?''

He rattled off the last numbers he remembered achieving. ''I can run the hundred-meter dash in ten seconds.''

Beth smiled as she clapped her hands together with relish. ''Excellent.'' He would do very nicely indeed.

The glint in her eye intensified. "How do you feel about helping Cupid along, Bryce?"

He crossed his arms at his chest and eyed her. "Just what is Cupid supposed to be doing?"

Beth dropped back into her winged chair, still looking up at him. Pleased with her plan. "Mugging someone."

Bryce shook his head. His grin was just slightly confused. "Come again?"

"I think, my dear, that a little live improvisational theater might be just what you need to keep you fresh and on your toes."

"And where is this live performance supposed to take place? Off-Broadway?"

Oh, it was off Broadway, all right, Beth thought. Way off. "The Metropolitan Museum of Art. More specifically, the alley beside it."

"All right, you've got me really curious now." He perched on the edge of the arm of her winged chair. "Fill in the blanks for me."

He was in on it, she could tell. It was what she liked best about him. His willing spirit. "With pleasure, my dear."

Matt didn't mind art. He had to admit that during the endless hours they'd spent crisscrossing the different rooms within the Metropolitan Museum of Art, Rose had shown him several pieces that he hadn't minded looking at. They were even nice—especially the one with water by Monet, or Manet, or something like that. The names were swimming in his head.

But if he were being totally honest with Rose as well as himself, what he liked best about the museum was its air-conditioning system.

What's more, he had a sneaking suspicion that at least half of the souls wandering around the museum today agreed with him.

Impatience drummed through him as he followed Rose to yet another painting; this one a mass of colors he could have sworn a three-year-old had created by getting into a paint box and flinging the contents onto a canvas.

Matt had moved slowly, just as Beth had counseled him to do. Trouble was, it was so slow that he was beginning to feel as if he were actually moving backward.

In addition, he still couldn't get the little nun's question out of his mind. It had planted a seed that he couldn't seem to weed out.

Is she pregnant?

He knew that it was ridiculous to even remotely entertain the idea, and yet he just couldn't seem to get past the question. It nagged him, cropping up at odd times in the day and night. Asking Rose would be nothing short of insulting, and he knew it. The logical conclusion to be drawn was that she'd fainted because of the heat.

Still, that little notion kept buzzing around his head.

What if she was pregnant?

What if that was the real reason Rose had left—because she couldn't face him?

That was absurd, too, he chided, because why shouldn't she face him? After all, if she was pregnant, it was his baby, too...

Unless it wasn't.

Abruptly, Matt shut his mind down, refusing to go any further with the thought. He was getting far too carried away with something that probably didn't have a germ of truth in it. Rose deserved better than that from him, he thought, annoyed with himself. And he should have better control over his own thoughts than to let his mind wander like that.

"So, what do you think?" she was asking. She'd stepped back from the painting she was admiring. And then she took a better look at Matt. Rose smiled. He'd been indulging her. "You're bored, aren't you?"

Matt tried not to blink like a man waking up from a self-induced trance.

"No," he lied.

He didn't lie worth a damn. Which was good in her book. "Then why are you trying to stifle a yawn?"

He shrugged carelessly, looking away at another painting. This one had slashes of red and yellow. "I didn't sleep much last night."

That much was true. He'd kept waking up all

through the night. Thinking of her. Wanting so badly to cut the distance between their two rooms and to get into her bed. He'd actually gotten up several times, only to herd himself back into his bed.

If he kept it up, Beth was going to have a path worn in her rug, he mused.

"Maybe we've had enough culture for one day." Rose glanced at her watch. She knew that the museum would be closing within the half hour. "It's getting a little late, anyway. What do you say we go back to Aunt Beth's and then maybe the three of us can go out to dinner?"

He'd much rather it was the two of them, but he kept that to himself.

Agreeable, be agreeable, he kept repeating silently. He was going to wear her down with his agreeableness or die in the attempt.

"Sure."

They'd worked their way down to the first floor again. Having spent the better part of the day here, Matt had gotten the lay of the museum pretty well memorized. He led the way to the front entrance.

He was a man who didn't ask directions, but he never seemed to need any. He'd always had an uncanny sense of direction, Rose mused.

There was so much about Matt that made him stand out from all the others. Sometimes, despite her resolution to keep her distance, she wanted to forget and just be with him. In the total sense of the word. She knew she'd be negating all the groundwork she'd made up, but it was getting harder and harder for her to be noble about this. Especially when she wanted nothing more than to have him hold her.

To have him make love with her.

The sad thing was that it looked as if he'd finally come to believe her that she didn't want any of that. They'd spent every day going somewhere new and he'd been a complete and utter gentleman. He'd faithfully observed rules one and two ever since she'd fainted in front of St. Patrick's Cathedral.

That had been a week ago and he hadn't tried anything. Not a single, solitary thing.

Maybe he really was here just to play tourist. Maybe he had lost interest in her.

The thought pinched her heart and her stomach. It was all for the best, she knew that, but it certainly didn't feel that way.

It felt as if someone had gutted her.

It felt, she thought, exactly the way it had when she'd screwed up her courage and lied to him, saying that she'd lost interest in their being together and that it was all for the best if they just didn't see each other anymore.

Maybe this was payback.

Maybe this was some elaborate charade Matt was orchestrating to let her see how it felt to be emotionally abandoned.

Maybe, Rose advised herself as they walked outside, she had better stop letting her imagination run away with her and just cease thinking altogether.

It felt as if she'd stepped into an oven. A hot, moist oven.

"Didn't get any cooler while we were inside, did it?" she murmured as the door sighed closed behind them.

He looked at her, concerned. "You're not planning to faint again, are you?"

"That was entirely unplanned," she assured him. "And I'd just as soon you didn't bring that up again."

They began to walk down the street. Several cabs went by, but they were either occupied or off duty.

"Why?"

She wondered if he was walking slower because he was tired, or because he didn't think she could keep up. Her sense of competition made her want to pick up the pace, but this baby kept sapping her strength.

"Because I'd rather not think of myself as one of those weak-wristed women who pass out."

He slanted a look at her and smiled. "Nothing weak about you. You've got a will of iron. I heard your aunt talking about someone she once knew who was nicknamed the Iron Butterfly. I kind of figure that name suits you pretty well."

It took her a second to sort through her aunt's stories in her head and make the connection. "That was Loretta Young's nickname."

The name meant nothing to him. "Who?"

She'd said the same thing the first time Aunt Beth had told her. Then spent the next two hours watching a video of *The Farmer's Daughter.* "A big-time actress my aunt met when she was first starting out. That was when Aunt Beth went to Hollywood. She got a part in Miss Young's TV show."

Matt could only shake his head. "Your aunt's certainly been around."

"That she has." Rose fought the temptation to slip her arm through his, even though it would have felt natural to do so. "I'm glad you like her."

"I like her niece better." Damn. It had just slipped out. He admonished himself, hoping it hadn't sent him back to square one. Beth had all but promised him that if he held back, Rose would come around. He could only hope the older woman knew what she was talking about. "Oh, sorry, I know I'm not supposed to say that."

She smiled. The compliment warmed her like the good wine she missed having on special occasions. "That's all right, I—"

Rose didn't get a chance to finish what she was saying. Still keeping an eye out for a cab, they'd crossed the street and were passing an alley. Someone grabbed her from behind and yanked her into the shadows.

"Just give me your money and the little lady doesn't get hurt," the attacker threatened.

Rose's eyes grew large as she became utterly still.

The scent of a man's cologne registered at the same time that fear made its appearance. She saw the look in Matt's eyes. There was instant pent-up fury there, as volatile as the tornadoes that periodically tore through the Texas Panhandle.

He was going to do something heroically stupid, she just knew it. If he got hurt defending her, she wouldn't be able to live with it.

"Here." Still unable to see her assailant, only smell him, Rose twisted her arm, thrusting her purse toward him. "Take it. Just go and leave us alone."

A long arm clad in a black sweater reached out around her and snatched the purse from her hand. He pushed her away from him, but far more gently than she would have anticipated.

Rose turned around, but she couldn't make out the mugger's features. He was wearing a black ski mask.

Out of the corner of her eye, she saw Matt make a move toward the mugger. She didn't want him hurt. "No, Matt," she cried. "Please, it's just money."

"It's *your* money," Matt growled as he lunged after the man.

The latter instantly pivoted on his heel, dropped the purse and took off.

Matt gave chase, but the man was faster than he was, dashing like an Olympic runner. Very quickly, he left an angry Matt far behind him. Matt knew it was useless to continue.

Embarrassed that he'd failed to catch the mugger,

Matt cursed roundly under his breath as he hurried back to Rose. He found her not far from where he'd left her, purse in hand. She was shaking and there were tears in her eyes.

Damn it, had that scum hurt her? With all his heart, he wished he'd caught him. He'd have made him pay.

"Are you all right?" He ran his hands over her arms just to reassure himself that there was nothing bruised or broken.

"Yes, I'm okay." And then she all but collapsed, but not out of fear for herself. Out of fear for him. "Oh, God, Matt, when I saw you take off after him—"

She couldn't finish.

Instead, she threw her arms around him and kissed him with every ounce of what she was feeling and what she had been feeling this past week.

Maybe virtue was its own reward, but this was certainly a hell of a lot nicer, Matt thought, his arms tightening around her. A hell of a lot.

The kiss deepened, taking Matt to places he had already been, places he had so desperately wanted to revisit.

Abruptly, stunned, trying to get her bearings, Rose stepped back. The next moment, she pulled back her fist and hit him in the chest as hard as she could.

Matt's hand went over his chest, far more out of bewilderment than from any sort of pain. "What was that for?"

She could feel fresh tears in her eyes. He was alive. But he might not have been. And he would have died thinking she didn't love him.

"He could have killed you," she cried.

"I didn't think he had a gun and he was pretty puny when you took a good look at him."

"But he *could* have had a gun," she emphasized. "Damn it, Matt, it was only my purse. And he dropped it. There was no reason to risk your life over it."

Didn't she get it? His hands on her shoulders, he looked into her eyes. "I wasn't risking my life over the purse, I was going after him because he'd put his hands on you. Because he could have hurt you and I couldn't stand that." He gently slid his knuckles along her cheek. "Nobody's got a right to manhandle you like that."

She melted, completely and utterly melted. Threading her arms around his neck again, Rose sealed her lips to those of the only man she had ever loved.

"Hey, get a room, you two," someone snickered as they hurried by.

It sounded like a plan to her.

Nine

Matt pulled his head back, away from Rose, though it wasn't easy. He would have been willing to remain there, kissing her until the twelfth of never, or until the cows came home, whichever happened last. But he knew that the longer he kissed her, the more he would want, and he'd promised himself he wasn't going to push.

"Maybe we should go somewhere else," he said huskily.

Rose pressed her lips together, savoring the taste of him. It wouldn't do, she thought ruefully, to say that the somewhere else she wanted to go was back to the apartment, to slip into her room and wait for him to come in once they were sure that Aunt Beth was either asleep or out for the evening.

It wouldn't do—but she wanted to. With all her heart, she wanted to.

He wanted to take her to her apartment and make love to her, so slowly that both of them would literally ignite from the heat of the anticipation. But saying so would probably scare her off, so instead, he went the safer route, hoping to lay further groundwork in the right direction.

"How about dinner, and then a ride around Central Park in one of those horse-drawn buggies like your aunt suggested?"

"Carriage tours," she corrected.

"Right." He took the correction in stride. "One of those."

She remembered that she'd originally suggested bringing her aunt along. She didn't want to anymore. But maybe he did. She slanted a look toward him. "With or without Aunt Beth?"

Matt touched her face softly, his eyes telling her the things that were in his heart, the way he couldn't yet. "What do you think?"

The smile came slowly, then picked up pace until her mouth curved completely. "I guess I'm not going home to change."

"Don't change a thing," he murmured against her ear. His hand to her back, Matt nudged her toward the curb, then his other hand shot up as he saw an available cab approaching in the distance. Leaving her on the curb, he got out in front of the vehicle before the cabbie had the opportunity to ignore him.

"You're starting to behave like a native," Rose noted with a laugh as the cab came to an abrupt halt.

Matt held the rear door open for her. "Hey, I'm flexible. Remember?" he whispered in her ear as she got in and sat down.

She slid over, making room for him. She remembered how flexible his body was when they'd made love. "I guess you are at that."

Flexible was definitely the word, she thought, going with the normal meaning. What other man would have swallowed his pride and followed her out here? Would have gone through the trouble of finding out where she was in the first place? Rose knew that her whereabouts weren't common knowledge, other than to her family. And she couldn't picture Matt waltzing up to the door of the Wainwright ranch house to ask her father or brother where she was. Not without sustaining bodily harm. Especially if either one of them should suspect that Matt and she had been sleeping together.

Which meant that he had to have gone to a lot of trouble to search her out.

The thought made her smile.

Matt cocked his head, trying to fathom the enigmatic look on her face. "What?"

"Just how did you find out where I was staying?"

He supposed he could make up something to impress her, but he'd always found that going with the truth was the simplest thing to do. Lies, even invented for a good cause, could trip you up later. He didn't want anything to trip him with Rose.

"From Daisy, that new bartender at the Lone Star Country Club's Men's Grill. When I asked if she'd seen you, she mentioned that you'd been there for a last look around before you went to New York. Then I remembered that you had an aunt living here.''

It had been a little more complicated than that, but he didn't want to go into it. There was no point in her knowing that he'd braved the Internet to find out where Beth lived. Or that it had taken him twelve tries to get the information.

Rose clearly was impressed. In her experience, most men didn't listen. ''And you remembered her name?''

He'd discovered that when he thought about it, he remembered everything that came out of Rose's mouth.

''I remember a lot of things,'' he said vaguely.

Even after several pep talks from Beth, Matt didn't know how much he should let Rose know and how much to hold back. Damn, but he hated these games. Hated being so unsure about his next move.

The only thing he knew for sure was that being away from Rose tore up his gut and hurt like hell. Did that mean that he was in love with her? The lasting kind of love that people built commitments on? That they built marriages on?

He didn't know.

Or maybe he did and was just too scared to admit it, even to himself.

Disgusted, the cabbie twisted around in his seat, pushing his N.Y. Mets cap far back on his head, revealing a large section of shining bald head.

"Look, I hate to break up this lovely conversation you two are having, but where to?" His hand was poised over the meter flag. He clearly intended to pull it down whether or not they were quick to give him a location.

Rose looked at Matt expectantly.

"Your choice," he said to her.

So far, they'd had Chinese food, Thai food, gone to a steak house, a seafood restaurant and sampled Cajun food. All, except the steak house, at her behest. It was his turn to choose, she thought.

"What do you feel like having, Matt?"

You, was his immediate response, but he made it silently. He knew that the answer wouldn't have gone over well at the moment, not with the beefy cabbie with two day's worth of beard on his face still leering at them. "Surprise me," Matt told her.

Thinking of the ride around the perimeter of Central Park, Rose gave the driver the name and address of a restaurant located near the Plaza Hotel, where the carriages usually clustered.

Settling back in her seat, she looked at Matt. "Tonight we're having Italian."

Tonight, he hoped, he was having her. If pressed, he could have recounted the seconds since they'd last made love. He hadn't known then that the following day she would be telling him that she was tired of their relationship, tired of him. She certainly hadn't acted tired of him that last afternoon they'd shared.

She'd been warm and supple in his arms, like sunshine that had been captured, only to be released to flow over every part of him.

She could hardly eat. Though she normally adored chicken tetrazzini, facing it in person and coaxing the forkfuls into her mouth turned out to be another matter. Rose felt as if her entire stomach had turned into one huge knot.

This time, she didn't think the baby had anything to do with it.

This time it was anticipation. It was as if she was a time bomb set to go off. She just didn't know where and she didn't know when. All she knew was that it involved Matt.

She glanced at him now. He'd almost finished his dinner. At least one of them could eat, she thought ruefully.

"How is everything tonight?" the slim-waisted, even slimmer-hipped waiter asked fifteen minutes after delivering their order. He looked at Rose's plate and his smile faded slightly. Hands joined together, he stopped just short of wringing them. "Is the meal not to your liking, ma'am?"

Someone had worked hard to prepare this. She looked at her plate, her sense of empathy kicking in and making her feel guilty.

"Oh, no, the meal is wonderful. Really," she added when he looked doubtful.

"I'm afraid I'm just not as hungry as I thought."

The waiter nodded. "I could have it wrapped up for you to take home," he offered.

She knew that Beth would enjoy this as a midnight snack, or have it first thing in the morning. Beth did not believe in traditional breakfast fare as the first meal of the day.

Rose gestured toward the plate. "That would be very nice, thank you."

"I guess you don't want dessert, then, either," Matt said.

Dessert made her think of ice cream. And ice cream reminded her of the time when they'd gone on a picnic and Matt had dribbled a little of his ice cream onto her arm, then licked it off.

Slowly.

Heat shot through her as if it had been fired from a well-aimed gun.

"Ice cream," she said suddenly, then looked at the departing waiter, who paused when he heard her place her order. "Please."

He smiled, inclining his perfectly combed head. "Certainly. What flavor?"

She tried not to look at Matt and wasn't sure if she was successful in her effort. "Vanilla."

Out of the corner of her eye, she thought she detected a hint of a smile on Matt's face, but she wasn't sure.

* * *

A full moon was out to greet them when they finally left the restaurant. The air was incredibly still. The stickiness that hugged the city had abated, but only marginally. It was a short walk to the Plaza Hotel, where they found a fleet of carriages with magnificently groomed horses and regally attired drivers all waiting to aid a couple in finding a romantic end to a wonderful evening.

Matt picked a carriage and held her hand as she climbed in before taking his place beside her.

All the sounds of the city took a back seat to the steady clip-clop of the chestnut bay's hooves along the path.

The gentle swaying of the carriage was incredibly soothing. Sitting beside Matt had the exact opposite effect for Rose. The two sensations complemented each other.

Rose let her guard down just enough to rest her head on Matt's shoulder. She sighed. This was perfect, just perfect.

"Did I thank you for saving me?" she asked, her voice dreamy.

"Twice." Unable to resist, he pressed a kiss to her forehead. She couldn't fault him for that, he reasoned. Not after she'd kissed him on the mouth earlier. "But you can do it again if it makes you feel good."

Rose stifled a giggle that came out of nowhere. She shifted her head to look up at him. Matt was smiling, just as she'd suspected. Without thinking, she reached up and traced his mouth with her fingertips, wanting to feel him.

Matt lightly caught her hand in his and pressed her fingers to his lips, kissing them one by one.

It was hard to stop her heart from hammering. She was positive he had to hear it. That would ruin everything. She didn't want to give up this evening, this fantasy, but she knew the danger that was involved. She couldn't allow herself to be taken too far into the fantasy, couldn't allow herself to believe that she could live happily ever after. That things could somehow work themselves out between a Wainwright and a Carson.

She dropped her hand in her lap. "Thank you," she murmured.

"Don't mention it." He kissed her forehead again, aching for her lips instead. "Unless you want to."

Rose laughed.

It felt good to laugh, to be with him here like this tonight. The heat and humidity faded into the background. All she was aware of, other than Matt, were the feelings that were swirling through her. Feelings that all involved him.

It was nice to know that she truly loved the father of her baby. That her baby was conceived, however unintentionally, in love. A baby conceived in love had a head start.

But what of the rest of it? a small voice asked.

What about after conception? After birth? What kind of a life can you give your baby then?

One filled with love, she insisted silently. Because no matter what, she loved her baby, had loved it from the first moment she'd known it was there, its tiny heart beating beneath hers. Forming beneath hers. She'd taken one of those home pregnancy tests and unconsciously fallen in love the instant the stick had turned blue.

His arm slipped around her shoulder, pulling her a little closer to him still. Ever since the mugging earlier, Rose had seemed like a different woman. Or rather, the same woman that he remembered from Mission Creek. The one who had snatched his heart away from him.

Part of him felt like finding the mugger and giving him a tip.

Matt had been quiet too long. Nestled in the crook of his arm, Rose could feel his eyes on her, studying her. What did he see? A woman who had walked out on him? A woman he was determined to win back because of his pride? Or a woman who meant something to him?

Don't go there, she warned herself. Stop evaluating, just enjoy the moment. Because the moment was all they really had.

"What are you thinking about?" Matt finally asked, his voice soft.

His question caught her by surprise. She knew she

couldn't tell him. Rose hunted for something acceptable to say to him, then glanced up. She had her answer.

"That the sky looks pretty tonight with all those stars."

He looked up himself. The stars were scattered like so many loose jewels. "Which one would you like?" he asked.

"Why?" She laughed. "Are you going to go out and lasso it for me?"

"No, I was thinking of something along the lines of ordering it for you from Neiman-Marcus."

She sat up, looking at him, knowing he meant diamonds. An engagement ring? Was he just joking or was he serious? Did he want to marry her because he loved her?

Or had he somehow learned about the baby?

She tried to find her answer in his expression and failed. "I don't need stars or diamonds."

As long as I have you, she thought, *even for just a little while longer.*

And then, when he said nothing further, she knew he was just talking, nothing more. That was all right, she counseled herself. She'd left Mission Creek not expecting anything more so this shouldn't have exactly been a surprise.

One day at a time, that was how she planned to take it. Just one day at a time. The rest would take care of itself. It would have to.

She didn't know when he was going home and until she knew, she could pretend that he wasn't. That moments like this, that feelings like this, would last forever instead of for just a little while.

And as long as she was away from home, from all the things she normally held dear and that dictated the path she had to walk in her life, these feelings *would* last forever.

The trick, she'd discovered, was not to think. At all.

"You got yourself a rare woman," the carriage driver said in a deep cockney accent. It went with the tall, stovepipe hat he wore. Turning, he winked at Matt to underscore his pronouncement.

"I already know that," Matt told him, looking down into Rose's face.

Unable to help herself, she placed her hand on his cheek, pulling his mouth down to hers. The kiss that flared between them was passion itself.

Her head began to spin instantly, the way it might have if she'd had wine with her meal. But she hadn't had a meal, hadn't had wine. Only ice cream.

Can you get intoxicated on ice cream? she wondered. Or was that the man who was doing this to her? Was it Matt who was scrambling the blood in her veins and the thoughts in her mind?

She didn't know, she didn't care. All she knew was that she liked this wild, heady feeling coursing through her and wanted more of it.

Most of all, she didn't want it to end.

"Okay, this is it, folks," the driver announced, accompanying his words with a loud, polite cough designed to force them apart. "We're back to where we started from."

Feeling more than slightly dazed, Rose pulled away and blinked, taking in the carriages lined up ahead of their horse. The majestic Plaza Hotel stood regally in the background.

"He's right," she murmured. A smattering of sadness slipped into her words.

Rather than step down, the driver looked at them over his shoulder, playing with the reins. "I could take you around again if you like, but it would be the same rate as before."

Matt was perfectly willing to continue going 'round in circles for the rest of the night, as long as she remained in his arms. Matt looked at her quizzically, but Rose shook her head.

There was someplace else that she wanted to be, someplace with secure walls, where no prying eyes could find them.

"Maybe next time," Matt told the man.

Matt slipped the driver a large tip and then got down off the carriage. He turned and placed his hands on Rose's waist to help her down.

The driver beamed at the bill he unfolded in his hand. "I'll be here," he promised.

But he was talking to himself. Matt and Rose were walking, arm-in-arm, toward the entrance of the apartment building where Beth lived—completely oblivious to Rule Number One.

Ten

The elevator doors parted and Rose stepped inside with Matt. Several other people got in with them, eating up the space and forcing them to stand close to each other. Extremely close.

The ride up in the elevator was the longest three minutes she'd ever endured.

Desire had already taken up residence within her and it was pulsating through every pore. Rose felt as if she would explode any second unless she got a chance to be alone with Matt.

Really alone.

Resolutions were all well and good if the man she was resolved never to be with again was a thousand miles away, safely out of sight if not out of mind.

But when he wasn't even one thousandth of an inch away, her resolve shredded faster than a wet tissue in a hurricane.

As it did now.

She would have liked to have blamed it on something—the moon, the carriage ride, his coming to her rescue. But it was none of these. It was him and the fact that she had never really even come close to getting over him and probably never would.

She knew that every time she looked into her child's face, she would see Matt.

Passengers trickled out on each floor. By the time they reached the twentieth, they were almost alone. As the elevator door slid open and they got off, Rose slipped her hand into his.

Matt looked into her eyes and knew that they were of like mind. The waiting was over. He wasn't sure what the step after the next one was going to entail, but he damn well knew what his very next step was going to be. Making love with her.

It was either that, or self-destruct. He'd come to the end of his control, the end of his restraint.

Unlocking the apartment door, praying that there would be no answer to her greeting, Rose called, "Aunt Beth, are you home?"

There was no reply.

Mentally, she crossed her fingers, knowing she shouldn't. Knowing that if they were alone in the apartment, the right thing for her to do would be to leave again. Because to stay would mean the inevitable.

She prayed for the inevitable.

Glancing at the marble table, Matt saw a sheet of notepaper with his and Rose's names written across the top in Beth's flowing hand. Scanning it, he smiled and blessed the woman for her foresight.

"Looks like we're alone." He held up the note. "She's gone to the theater for the evening. To see a revival of *My Fair Lady* and to a party afterward. Won't be home until after midnight."

He let the note fall from his fingers, his eyes intent on Rose's face. They were alone. Finally, completely alone.

Her breath grew short. "I guess that means we have the run of the place."

Suddenly nervous, she took a step back, her shoulders coming in contact with the wall. She looked at him, her heart beating in double-time.

His eyes holding her prisoner, Matt reached for the first button on her blouse and slowly slipped it from its hole. "I guess."

Desperate to say something, not wanting him to know that she was so eager for him that she was almost jumping out of her skin, Rose mumbled, "What would you like to do?" The words were thick as they left her lips.

The second button was freed, and then the third. His smile slipped over his lips as easily as the buttons slipped out of their holes.

"You guess."

She swallowed, but there was no moisture to be had within her mouth. It had gone drier than sand. "How many chances do I get?"

The blouse undone, he tugged it out of the waistband, then pressed a single kiss to her throat. He felt her pulse beating wildly beneath his lips.

"Depends." He raised his head to look at her. "How many will you need?"

Anticipation danced along her body like a ballerina whirling out of control.

"Shut up and kiss me," she ordered, unable to wait a single second longer.

Catching her hands and holding them above her head, against the wall, Matt threaded his fingers through hers as he pressed his body against hers. The heat that shot through him was like a long-lost, dearly missed old friend.

"Yes, ma'am," he said, a sliver of humor curving his mouth one second before desire chased it away.

His mouth came down on hers, dissolving any further words, any further thoughts, save one. That he wanted her. Wanted her the way he wanted air to sustain himself. Wanted her more.

Over and over again, his mouth slanted across hers, his body trapping her between him and the wall. Releasing her hands, he let his roam her sides, reveling in the familiar feel.

Reveling in the homecoming.

Damn, but he had missed her. He hadn't realized just how much until this very moment. Until desire all but threatened to completely shred him apart.

His mouth curved again as he felt her hands urgently race over him, tugging at the ends of his shirt, trying to loosen it in the negligible space that existed between their bodies.

He was vaguely aware of taking a half step back from her to allow Rose room to work. To allow himself space to do the same.

An urgency Rose could not begin to harness assaulted her as she almost ripped all the buttons off his shirt. They wouldn't undo easily and she was eager to touch his chest.

To feel his flesh against hers.

Her mouth still sealed to his, she finally managed to pull his shirt off his shoulders, doing so at the same time that he slipped her blouse from hers.

She shivered even though she had never been this warm before.

And then she felt the clasp between her shoulder blades being undone.

The next moment her bra straps were sliding down off her trembling shoulders and then the bra itself peeled from her breasts. It fell to the floor between them.

Fire licked the center of her very core as she felt the light hairs on Matt's chest slide against her breasts.

The next instant he was coaxing her skirt down over her hips until finally, all she was left wearing was a small scrap of white lace.

Rose felt more than saw Matt sink to his knees in front of her, his mouth pressing a hot trail of open-mouthed kisses from her waist down to where her lacy underwear met her quivering abdomen.

She sucked in her breath as his lips went lower, kissing her through the material.

And then he was tugging the material away.

Rose felt the final barrier slide down her thighs slowly, was consumed by the fire he was generating as his mouth took possession of what had already been his.

Groaning, she buried her fingers in his hair, pressing him closer. Biting back a moan before it turned into a scream.

Her body grew damp despite the air-conditioning.

Her breath completely vanished as Matt thrust his tongue in between her legs, bringing her to a climax before she even knew she was on the verge of having one.

The shudder went through her entire body.

Moist, stunned, she tried to focus as she felt herself being swept up into his arms.

Reacting, she threaded her arms around his neck and cleaved to him. She was still throbbing as he carried her to her room.

To her bed.

Laying her down gently, Matt quickly pulled off his trousers, kicking them aside before he began to shuck his underwear.

Watching him, her eyes wide, she whispered, ''No. Let me do it.''

Her husky voice traveled the length of his body, exciting him.

"Always glad to oblige."

Matt lay beside her, struggling to hold himself in check as he felt her cool fingers urge the cotton material from his hips. The path was impeded by the swell of his desire.

He closed his eyes, absorbing her touch as her palm lightly glided over him before she continued pulling the material ever downward. And then, changing gears, she swiftly yanked his briefs down his legs and tossed them aside.

Matt saw the glint in her eyes. She would have slowly dragged the length of her body over his, tantalizing him to the breaking point, but he pulled her to him, need preventing him from patiently waiting for contact.

Fitting her against his body, he raised his head and caught her lips. With his hand to the back of her neck, he held her in place as his mouth savaged hers.

It was then he knew that he would never get enough of her.

The more he kissed her, held her, touched her, the more he needed to.

Shifting so that it was her back against the bed instead of his, Matt reined himself in enough so that he could re-explore terrain that he was already achingly familiar with.

So that he could reclaim all that had once been his.

Beneath him, Rose twisted and turned, eager to feel, eager to experience. With each pass of his hand, each kiss he pressed to her skin, she grew more and more excited, wanting it to go on forever.

Wanting to take the final plunge.

The opposing desires warred with each other, just as they had all along. There was no resolution. All she knew was that she was just barely holding on to the precipice by her fingertips and that if they didn't come together soon, she wouldn't be responsible for her actions.

He made love to every part of her, glorying in the silky feel of her.

Grateful for the second chance.

She was his.

No matter what she said to deny it, he knew she was his. She'd surrendered herself to him at the very first touch. And it humbled him and filled him with joy at the same time.

Passion all but burned away the sheets that tangled beneath them as first he led the way, then she did, each taking a turn at dazzling the other. At being the jailer and the jailed.

Sweat slicking her body, her heart pounding almost beyond its limit, Rose looked up at him.

"Please."

He hardly heard the word. It was more as if it was echoing in his brain, in his soul.

The smile that came to his lips was soft, sensitive.

"Never ask for what you already have," he whispered against her cheek.

And then, raising himself up on his elbows, Matt parted her legs with his own and slid into her, at first gently, then with increasing urgency. Sheathed within her, he caught her hands with his own, and held them above her head.

His eyes on hers, satisfying himself that she felt the same desire, the same sense of urgency mingled with contentment that he did, Matt began to move. At first slowly, then faster and faster until it seemed as if the whole world was moving to a wild, furious tempo that had seized their bodies within its grip.

Rose cried out his name as she felt herself being hurled first up and then over the summit.

As Matt sank down against her, his breathing labored, she knew that he had reached the peak at the same time she had.

The knowledge made her smile.

Whatever happened after tonight would be all right, she thought. She could handle it because she had this to remember.

And this time had been the best time.

Exhausted, Matt began to shift his weight from her, but he felt her arms tighten around him.

"Not yet," she told him, so tired she could hardly form the words, but unwilling to lose the moment. "Wait a minute longer."

"A minute longer and it'll be shorter," he murmured against her cheek, grinning as he brushed a kiss there. "Wouldn't want to be embarrassed in your presence," he teased, shifting to the side. He slipped his arm around her and pulled her closer.

She clung to the rosy afterglow surrounding her. "Trust me, you will never have anything to be embarrassed about."

He raised himself up on one elbow and leaned his head on his fisted hand, looking down at her. "Oh, and you've made a study of this, have you?"

He'd been her first and they both knew that. And her last. That was something she alone knew. Because there'd never be anyone like him in her life again.

"No, it's just something a woman just knows," she told him.

He laughed, his fingers lightly stroking her breasts. "Just make sure you don't decide to do any extensive research on the subject," he warned. His grin widened as he saw her nipples harden beneath his hand. He rubbed his thumb against one peak, enjoying the way she moved in response. "Chilly?"

Silently she moved her head from side to side in denial, desire creeping up her toes like a hot ray of sunshine taking possession of the land. A moment ago she could have sworn that she barely had the strength for breathing. And yet here it was, out of the blue: desire. All dressed up and ready to go to town again.

What *was* it he did to her? "Just the opposite."

Matt raised a brow, amused. He gathered her to

him, his body already hardening in anticipation. "Got a fire you need putting out?"

She turned her body into his. "Think you're man enough to do it?"

Catching her earlobe between his teeth, he suckled it before saying, "Man and a half."

Never in her wildest dreams did she think that any man could have her burn so brightly. She'd just finished making love with him and all she could think about was doing it again. And again.

"Think a lot of yourself, do you?"

"Actually, it's you I'm thinking of." He wove his fingers through her hair, brushing it from her face. "You could raise the dead if you wanted to, Rose. And make a celibate man forget his vows."

She laughed, curling her body into his. "Oh, like you were ever celibate."

He felt himself becoming more and more aroused. "Never said it was me. But I have been," he told more seriously. "Since you."

She thought her heart would burst with the surge of love she felt.

Taking his face between her hands, Rose lightly framed it with her fingers as she raised her head to press her lips against his.

And to begin the second round of what was to be a three-round match that night.

Moving on tiptoes, Beth slowly closed the door behind her. The play had been wonderful, the company divine, although she had to admit that time and again, her thoughts strayed to what might be happening within her apartment while she was gone.

The lights, she noted, had been left on in the living room. She wondered if that meant they were still up and out here.

She'd hoped...

Beth stopped dead as she turned to place her purse on the marble table.

Her note wasn't where she'd left it. Instead, it was on the floor. Beside the blouse she remembered that Rose had been wearing. Which was beside Matt's shirt.

A wide grin graced her lips.

Finally, Beth thought, closing her eyes. Hallelujah! She had begun to give up hope that those two would ever get together again.

Whistling the chorus from "Getting To Know You," she bent and picked up the two shirts. Her tune changed to "We're Having a Heat Wave," when she saw Rose's skirt. Picking it up and tucking it on top of the shirts, she felt that this showed real promise.

And then she spied Rose's underwear a short distance away. She began whistling "Love is Lovelier the Second Time Around."

Humming, Beth scanned the area to see if she could find Matt's trousers or underwear. She didn't. No matter, she decided. They could have very easily been shed in whichever bedroom they'd wound up in, Rose's or his.

Depositing the clothing she'd gathered on the back of a nearby armchair, Beth made a mental note to find a way to slip the garments into the appropriate rooms in the wee hours of the night.

No sense in embarrassing the lovebirds, she thought. She just wanted them nesting properly.

Or improperly as the case was, she corrected herself. The rectangular mirror in the hallway caught her wide grin and flashed it back at her.

For the evening, her work was done. Content, Beth went off to bed.

Eleven

Oh, no, not now.

The frantic thought assaulted Rose just as the churning in her stomach rudely yanked her out of the land of misty dreams and warm contentment.

Please not now. Not when he was here sleeping beside her.

Bunching the sheet beneath her hands, her knuckles all but white, Rose lay in bed, desperately trying to project her mind elsewhere. Or, if not her mind, then at least her stomach.

But the more she tried, the worse it became. Within two minutes of waking, she knew that if she didn't get out of bed and fast, she was going to throw up right here, right now.

That would have been a hell of a spectacle for Matt to wake up to.

Watching him carefully, Rose slid her feet out first. Matt didn't move.

Not wasting time on a sigh of relief, she got up quickly, then padded as silently as she could across the carpet. Rose grabbed the thin cotton robe she had thrown over the back of the footboard the other night.

She pressed her lips together, willing herself not to throw up until she got into the bathroom. Perspiration beaded on her brow and for a moment, it was touch and go, but she made it.

Once there, she shut the door as quietly and quickly as she could and jammed her arms through the sleeves of the robe. The thought occurred to her that if she died here, she didn't want to be found nude.

Rose barely got the robe on before she fell to her knees in front of the commode. Just in time.

This bout, she immediately realized with the first wave that hit, was going to be worse than the others.

She was right. This one felt as if her entire body was being turned inside out.

Tears came to her eyes and her throat felt like rawhide. Each time she thought she was finished, there was more. And when there wasn't more, her insides still went through the motions until she thought she was just going to die there, clutching the sides of the white porcelain bowl and heaving.

It was a hell of a way to celebrate having a baby.

A light, early morning breeze quietly tiptoed into the bedroom, seeking shelter from the hot, humid day that was already forming. It gently skipped along Matt's barely covered torso, stirring him into a state of semiwakefulness.

With a sigh that went miles beyond mere contentment, Matt turned, his eyes still closed, and reached for Rose. He wanted to gather her to him and to sustain this feeling drifting through him for as long as he possibly could. Last night had been perfect and he intended for it to be the first of many perfect evenings that they would spend together. Feuding families notwithstanding, there was no earthly reason why they couldn't find a way to work things out if they tried hard enough.

The next moment, his eyes opened to confirm what his senses already told him.

She wasn't there.

Disappointed, still a little dazed from sleep, Matt raised his head and looked around the room, wondering why she would slip out of bed without waking him.

When he saw the closed bathroom door, he had his answer.

Sitting back against the pillows, he laced his fingers together behind his head. He planned to be ready for her when Rose slipped back under the covers. Ready and waiting. Just remembering last night was getting him aroused.

The sight of her supple, soft body, the gleam of the sweat created between their two bodies...

The strange muffled noise caught his attention.

Sitting up, Matt listened intently. It was coming from the bathroom. If he didn't know better, he would have said that it sounded as if someone was being sick.

It *was*.

Rose?

Worried, Matt swung his legs out of bed and got up quickly. The retching noise continued. Could she have gotten food poisoning last night?

He stopped beside the bathroom door for half a second to consider the thought.

He and Rose had had identical dinners last night, right down to the sparkling cider. He'd wanted something stronger, but when she told him she didn't feel like having wine, he'd gone along with her choice, determined to be in harmony with her all evening. Now that he thought about it, she hadn't had a drop of alcohol at any of the meals they'd had since he'd come to New York. He remembered her saying that she'd read that having a glass of wine at dinner was actually healthy for you. Why had she changed her mind?

And for that matter, he recalled, Rose had barely eaten her dinner. She'd toyed with it and had perhaps no more than a couple of bites. If there was food poisoning involved, he should have been the one to come down with it, not her.

But he didn't feel sick.

On the other hand, if that noise coming from the bathroom was any indication, Rose sounded utterly miserable. He wondered if he should go get Beth.

Doubling back to the bed, he picked up the trousers he'd shed last night. Foregoing any underwear for the time being, Matt pulled his pants on and tugged the zipper up as he crossed back to the bathroom door.

He knocked lightly. Abruptly, the noise stopped. Matt leaned against the door. What was going on? "Rose, are you all right?"

Oh, God, Rose thought, he'd heard her.

Thoroughly miserable, Rose covered her mouth to hold back the squeal of distress.

"Fine," she managed to call as she dragged herself up to her wobbly feet.

As quickly and quietly as she could, she turned on the water and then cupped her hands together beneath the faucet. Rose took a quick drink of the water that pooled into her joined palms. Swishing the water around, she spat it out again.

Her mouth felt terrible, as did the rest of her. But at least she'd stopped throwing up. For today.

He frowned. "You don't sound fine. Was it last night's dinner?"

"Yes." She wiped her face, clutching at the excuse. "I guess so. I mean, well..." she couldn't force herself to elaborate. "Maybe."

The next minute Matt opened the door. Beads of perspiration had plastered her hair to her forehead. Just like last night, he recalled. But last night she hadn't looked this miserable, despite the brave smile she was trying to put on now.

For a second he just stood there, not certain if he was encroaching on her space. He knew that whenever he was sick, he just wanted to be left alone. But he couldn't just walk out on her.

"Is there anything I can do?"

She shook her head. Slowly. Afraid of beginning the process all over again.

"No, not unless you'd like to throw up for me." She flashed him as bright a smile as she could muster under the circumstances. "I'm okay now. Really."

He touched her forehead to see if it was warm. It wasn't, but it was certainly damp. And her cheeks were flushed again.

Just the way they had been when she'd fainted last week.

The scene nagged at him. As did the question Sister Mary Katherine had asked him when she'd first seen Rose slumped in his arms at St. Patrick's Cathedral.

Rose pulled her head back from his hand. "I'm all right," she insisted.

And then she saw the look in his eyes. It was a strange look, as if he was seeing her for the first time. It made her uneasy and she debated pretending not to notice. But she couldn't just ignore the question in his eyes. She'd resolved to meet life head-on, and Matt was part of life.

"What?" she said.

Matt felt foolish asking, but he knew it wouldn't give him any peace until he put it to rest. Amid the uneasiness was an apprehensiveness, as well. What she would say in reply could very well change his life.

Both their lives.

Matt forced the words out before he thought better of it. "Rose, are you pregnant?"

She went deathly pale. He'd asked the one question she'd feared ever since she'd seen him standing on her aunt's doorstep. She couldn't lie, but she couldn't tell him the truth, either.

She stalled. "What makes you ask something like that?"

Rose hadn't hotly denied his question. If she wasn't pregnant, she would have. He had his answer. It wasn't an answer he wanted or knew what to do with.

But she looks so thin, his mind protested. He'd touched her, ran his hands all along her body last night. She didn't seem any different than she had back home, except perhaps to be even more amorous. She couldn't possibly be pregnant.

Could she?

"You are pregnant, aren't you?"

It wasn't in Rose to lie. Evade, yes, for dear life the way she had her father's questions, but not lie outright. She never had, to anyone, least of all to someone who meant so much to her. If her father had asked her if Matt Carson was the father of her baby, she would have had no choice but to say yes.

Just as she had no choice here.

But you lied to him when you told him you wanted

to go your own way, a small voice inside her head insisted. *You didn't want to, you had to.* And that, she knew, had been her way out. Semantics.

There were no semantics to play with here. Only a direct question, a direct assumption.

Squaring her shoulders, Rose looked at Matt, the unwitting father of her baby. She was a soldier facing the enemy. "Yes, I am."

Despite the fact that he thought he knew her answer, when she gave it, it hit him right in the gut like an exploding torpedo.

"Why didn't you say something?" he demanded, the numbness giving way to anger.

She didn't like the tone he was taking. He made it sound as if she owed him daily reports on her activities. "That's obvious," she retorted. "Because I didn't want you to know."

There was only one reason for that as far as he could see. And it hurt more than that time he'd been thrown from his horse and had cracked three ribs.

"Whose is it?" he asked heatedly.

Her eyes widened so much that they hurt. How *could* he? "What?"

He was so angry, he didn't hear the dangerous note in her voice. Didn't see anything but what he took to be his own betrayal. "I want to know, Rose. I have a right to know." It took all he had for him not to grab her by her shoulders and shake her. "Who's the baby's father?"

Now he sounded just like her father. Except that her father hadn't all but blatantly accused her of being an unfaithful little whore. But that was exactly what Matt was saying to her.

She felt a flash of fury rise up in her breasts. "How dare you ask me that?"

"How dare I?" he thundered. "How dare I? I'll tell you how dare I. I 'dare' because I'm the poor, dumb fool who came all the way out here to talk you into coming back with him." The hurt was so bad it threatened to choke him completely. He couldn't think straight. "Because I'm the idiot who fell for a Wainwright when I should have known better."

It was the final blow. She thought the feud was absurd, but no one, not even Matt, was going to throw rocks at her family.

"'The idiot who fell for a Wainwright'?" she echoed. "You make it sound as if being a Wainwright is only second to having leprosy," Rose shouted at him. "Is that how you feel?"

He knew he'd made a mistake, knew he should apologize, but he was too hurt, too stunned to make amends. "I don't know what the hell I feel anymore."

"Well, I do. I feel angry. Damn angry that I wasted any time thinking about you, worrying about you—" Worrying about the way knowing that she was going to have his baby would affect him.

"Worrying about me?" He scowled at her. Now

what was she talking about? "Why the hell would you be worrying about me?"

She grasped the ends of her robe and tied them together. "Because I'm the idiot here, not you, that's why." She wasn't about to explain anything to him, not when he took that tone with her, not when he thought what he thought. Marching out of the bathroom, she pointed toward her bedroom door. "Now get the hell out of here. I mean it. Now!"

He wasn't about to go anywhere, not until he found out what he needed to know. "Not before you tell me the name of the snake I'm supposed to kill for crawling into your bed and making love to my woman."

Her mouth fell open. Now he was talking about her as if she were some kind of a possession, to be locked away with his precious rifles and the other inanimate objects that he collected.

"Your woman? Since when was I ever 'your' woman? All you ever said was that what we had between us was casual, that it was just a fling."

Those were the words that echoed in her head as she'd packed up to leave Mission Creek. You didn't burden a man who wanted no ties with the advent of a baby. Not unless you wanted to imprison both of you.

He snorted. "Well, you sure took me at my word, didn't you?"

Her chin shot up defiantly. "The word of a liar," she jeered. "Yes, I guess I did at that."

He wanted to take her and shake her. Wanted to press her to him and to demand to know why she was so bent on breaking his heart.

But he couldn't.

He couldn't make himself weak in her eyes and let her see that he still loved her even after she'd gone to someone else's bed.

The best thing would be if he just walked out of her room now and kept on walking. But he couldn't. Not while this fury raged through him.

Unable to help himself, Matt caught her by the shoulders, struggling not to give her at least one good shake. "Tell me who the bastard is and I'll cut his heart out and give it to you on a platter."

Her eyes narrowed into slits. For two cents she'd spit the answer at him. But she knew he'd given her the way out. If she still wanted it. If he believed that the baby belonged to someone else, he'd leave. They'd never see each other again and that would be the end of it. Just as she'd originally planned.

So why the hell did it hurt worse than if someone had just put a red-hot poker against her heart?

"You have no right to talk to me like that, no right to question me. Now get the hell out of my room!" she ordered. When he didn't move, she smacked the flat of her hand against his chest and pushed him through the door.

Right into Aunt Beth.

Summoned by the sound of raised voices, Beth looked at the two with confusion and concern etched into her well-moisturized face.

"You two are so loud, St. Patrick's Cathedral just called and asked if we want a priest to come and perform an exorcism." Beth looked from one angry face to the other. "What in heaven's name is going on here?"

"Ask him." Rose jerked a thumb at Matt. "He seems to have all the answers."

With that, Rose slammed the door on both of them and walked away.

The second the door closed, Beth saw Matt's shoulders lose their rigidity. Empathy flooded through her like Hurricane Andrew through Florida. She gave him an understanding smile.

"Would you like to come into the kitchen for a cup of coffee?"

He sighed. Matt shrugged carelessly, turning. "Sure. Could you lace it with some arsenic?"

"Now, now, it can't be as bad as all that—" And then she confided, "Although I have to admit it did sound pretty bad there for a minute." She walked into the kitchen, flipping on the overhead cam lights. "Woke me from a sound sleep."

"Sorry," he apologized.

"No apology necessary. At least," she amended, "not to me."

She laid her hand on his shoulder and gently forced him down into a chair at the kitchen table.

"Stay," she ordered humorously, then turned to the business at hand. Ada wasn't due in until almost ten, which coincidentally was around the time she got up in the morning. But coffee wasn't about to get itself. If she wanted it, she was going to have to find the coffee filters.

Selecting a set of cupboard doors, Beth began her quest. She hadn't a clue where most things in her kitchen were shelved.

"All right," she said cheerfully as she continued her search. "Do you want to tell me what that shouting match back there was all about?"

Staring down at his hands, he said darkly, "I found out that Rose is pregnant."

Beth halted her search for a second, glancing over her shoulder at Matt. "Oh."

"You knew?" he asked, stunned. Did everyone know? The thought only succeeded in making him feel that much more of a fool.

She waved a vague hand, dismissing the fact. Not bothering to tell him that she'd read it in Rose's face within the first half hour of her arrival. Sooner, actually. "Anyone with eyes would know—" She looked at him again, then smiled benevolently. "Except maybe a man," she amended.

Men were a whole different breed than women, she

thought. They didn't pick up on sensitive things such as this, at least not easily.

Matt didn't know if that was supposed to make him feel better or not and made no response. He was suddenly too miserable. How could Rose do this? How *could* she? he silently demanded.

"Here we are," Beth announced, breaking into his thoughts. She held the filters up like a trophy. Placing the box on the counter, Beth turned toward the refrigerator. At least she knew where the coffee was kept. "All that shouting couldn't have been because you found out she was pregnant. How did you find out, by the way?"

Matt shrugged. What did it matter how he found out? The point was that Rose was pregnant. "Rose was in the bathroom, throwing up. I woke up and heard her."

"That'll do it." Beth nodded absently as she measured out what she hoped was the proper amount of coffee grinds. "What made you think she was pregnant in the first place? I mean, she could have just been sick, right?"

"She fainted last week in front of St. Patrick's Cathedral. The nun that came out to help us asked me if Rose was pregnant."

Rose had failed to mention the fainting spell to her. Beth frowned. *That girl needs to be taking more prenatal vitamins,* she thought.

"I see. So now you know." She poured water into

the coffeepot and deposited that in turn into the coffee machine. "Why were you shouting at her?"

A fresh surge of fury went through him. "Because it's not mine."

Beth turned from the coffeemaker, stunned at his deduction. "Why wouldn't it be yours?"

He thought that was rather obvious. He'd come to his conclusion the only way he knew how. "She didn't tell me, so I thought…"

All Beth could do was shake her head. "Matt, Matt, Matt." She ruffled his hair. "You know, for a bright young man, you can be awfully stupid. Even for a Carson." He jerked his head up, indignant at the unexpected slam, only to see her smiling at him in satisfaction. "See? Doesn't feel very good when the arrow's piercing *your* hide, does it?" She saw that he was confused. "I came in on the argument when you made that remark about falling for a Wainwright."

Embarrassed, ashamed for being caught and for saying it in the first place, he shrugged.

"Sorry, I didn't mean anything by it. Just my temper getting the better of me. I thought she'd found someone else," he explained helplessly. The thought had instantly eaten away at his stomach. "That maybe she was seeing the two of us all the time and found out she was pregnant with his baby."

Beth sighed, setting down the two cups she'd taken from the cupboard. She held up one finger. "Number one, my boy, Don't jump to conclusions so quickly." She peered at him, trying to get at the truth without revealing anything she shouldn't. "Did Rose say there was another man?"

"No," he said miserably. "But she didn't say there wasn't. Wouldn't she have denied it if there wasn't another man?"

The secret was Rose's to disclose, not hers. Her hands were tied. Or, in this case, her lips. It was going to be hard to maintain the peace and still convince Matt to stick around. Sometimes she thought she could just shake that girl.

She held up another finger. "Number two, never assume anything. Wait to be given evidence. And number three, even if there had been two of you and she found herself pregnant after being with each— and I'm not saying that there is or was another man— there'd be no way of telling whose the baby was until afterward when the tests were performed, now would there?"

Feeling both betrayed by Rose and angry at himself for losing his temper Matt dropped his head into his hands.

"I guess I'm just not thinking clearly," he said.

"No, I guess you're not." Realizing she'd forgotten one of the more important components in coffee-making, she quickly placed the coffeepot beneath the spout just in time. The black liquid began to flow.

Content, Beth turned to look at him. "So now what are you going to do next?"

Logically, he should leave. He knew that. But logic gave way to a sense of wanting to protect Rose. It shot his common sense all to hell.

"There's only one thing I can do next," he told her. "I'm going to ask Rose to marry me. She can't come home as an unwed mother. I don't care how sophisticated the times are, there's still a stigma attached to an unwed mother where we come from. I can't let her go through that. Rose deserves better."

Yes, Beth thought, she does. And she had a sneaking suspicion that her niece was about to get exactly what she deserved—as long as Rose wasn't too stubborn and messed it up.

Twelve

"Keep your nose out of it, unless you want to find yourself looking at a price tag that's too high for you to pay."

As suddenly as it came, the voice disappeared. Judge Carl Bridges found himself listening to a dial tone droning in his ear. He realized that his hand was shaking visibly. They were getting to him.

He forced himself to replace the receiver. Early evening shadows were beginning to drift into his study. He stood alone in the encroaching darkness.

What did that make now, three calls? No, four. Four phone calls to his Mission Creek home with vaguely worded threats that no one but he could understand. He didn't have to ask what the "it" the gravelly voiced man on the other end of the line had been referring to. He knew.

He was being warned to stay clear of anything that had to do with the Texas mob. He supposed they thought that judges weren't immune to fear.

They were right.

It was obvious to him that someone had to have seen him visiting Isadora Mercado, Haley's mother, in the hospital just before she was murdered. There was no doubt in his mind that the woman he had once loved, the woman he loved still, had not expired because of complications due to the beating she'd received at the hands of someone affiliated with the mob. She had been murdered in her bed. Smothered. As a warning to her husband Johnny. You never walked away from the mob. It wouldn't let you.

Carl was only glad that he'd managed to get word to Haley and to sneak her into the hospital room to see her mother before Isadora was killed.

But it was apparent now that his simple act of kindness had placed him in jeopardy. That went double for Haley.

He could only hope that the FBI continued to keep her safe.

Carl tried to tell himself that if the Texas mob meant to kill him, they would have done it by now. But he knew them, knew what they were like. Toying with their intended victims was typical of their ruthless sense of humor. He was the mouse to their cat. It was as simple as that.

He didn't know if going to the FBI with his suspicions about the phone calls would even get him anywhere, much less the protection he knew he needed. He doubted that even with a wiretap the calls could be traced. The mob was too smart for that.

Still, he was a judge and had some pull.

Maybe it was worth a call at that. What did he have to lose?

But when he reached for the receiver again, it wasn't to put in a call to the nearest FBI office, it was to set his life in long overdue order. His sense of mortality haunted him like a dark, uninvited guest. If he were to die tonight, within the next hour, matters between him and Dylan, his estranged son, would remain unresolved for all time.

The situation had to be rectified. He couldn't die with that on his conscience. Couldn't die without Dylan knowing that he'd forgiven him all the sins of his past.

Pressing numbers on the keypad Carl had thought he'd long since forgotten, he called Dylan's number at his home.

The phone rang five times. Carl debated hanging up before some answering machine picked up. After all this time, he didn't want his first contact with Dylan to be in the form of a disembodied voice on an answering machine.

Better that than nothing, Carl told himself fatalistically. The phone rang another two times.

"Hello?"

Carl gripped the receiver. It wasn't an answering machine. It was Dylan. He took a deep breath. "Hello, Dylan?"

"Yes?" There was a pause on the other end of the line. Recognition failed to set in. "Who is this?"

Part of Carl wanted to hang up, to postpone this awkward call. But he was stronger than that. "Dylan, this is your father."

"Dad?" Dylan asked incredulously. The uncertainty in his voice indicated that he was trying to discern if this was some kind of a cruel joke.

Carl began to talk quickly, knowing if he didn't, it would never come out. He didn't want to give Dylan a chance to hang up. After all this time, his son had the right. The fault lay with him, not Dylan. He should have been more understanding, not so preoccupied about his image, about how it looked for a judge to have such a delinquent as a son.

But all that was in the past. Dylan had changed, reformed. Begun a new life. It was time to heal the scabs.

"Yes, it's me. Dylan, I don't remember what it was we argued about, what finally drove us apart, but I just want to say I'm sorry for my part. No," he amended with feeling, "I'm sorry for all of it. And sorry that it's taken you away from me for all this time."

There was silence on the other end. Silence that lasted so long, Carl wasn't sure if his son was still there.

And then he heard, "Dad, are you all right?"

There was concern in Dylan's voice. Carl felt an overwhelming sense of relief.

"Maybe I'm more all right now than I have been for a long time."

Genuine concern clicked in. "Dad, do you want me to come and get you? Where are you?"

The questions amused Carl. Dylan had to be thinking that he was going senile. But the truth was, he was thinking more clearly now than he had been all along.

"I'm home, Dylan."

Home. The word conjured up a plethora of memories for Dylan. Maybe, he thought as he began a dialogue with his father, it was time that home was more than just a memory, more than just a word. Maybe it was time to see it again for himself.

Matt couldn't shake off the feeling. He felt exactly like the feline in the title of the revival play to which Beth had given him and Rose tickets. *Cat on a Hot Tin Roof*. That was him, all right. An antsy creature unable to find a foothold or a place to stand. That was him when it came to his dealing with Rose.

He could hear Beth's words echoing in his head when she'd given him the tickets after he'd told her that he was going to propose to Rose.

Find a good place to do it, a public place where she can't yell at you. Although why a woman would yell at the man who had just pledged to give her his heart for all eternity was beyond him.

Hell, the whole gender of women was beyond him.

He didn't begin to pretend to understand any of them, least of all the woman who had lassoed his heart and then tied him up so tight, it would take steel bull cutters to set him free.

As they walked out of the Helen Hayes Theater, a mosquito buzzed around his head. Matt waved it away. The mosquito, he noticed, didn't want to have anything to do with Rose.

Rather than take the arm he'd offered her, Rose was walking alongside of him. He made the best of the situation, telling himself she'd come around.

"Did you like the play?" he asked, making conversation.

The question brought the first smile to her lips he'd seen all evening.

"I have always liked the play," she told him, recalling when as a six-year-old she'd first watched Paul Newman and Elizabeth Taylor on a late-night television movie. "Almost as much as that mosquito seems to like you."

He muttered under his breath, waving away a second one that circled around his head higher than the first.

"It's your sweet blood they're after." Her grin grew wider. "Some people attract mosquitoes more than others. I guess there's no accounting for taste."

"I notice they leave you alone," he observed darkly.

"As long as I'm with you, I'm safe." Rose laughed.

This had been a very enjoyable evening and she was feeling magnanimous. That Matt was still here considering what he thought about her surprised her. But she knew he had to be getting back to the ranch. It could only spare him for so long. Everything would all turn out for the best. In the interim, she could pretend that things were different. What was the harm? At most, they had a few days left.

"You're my own personal insect repellent," she told him.

That didn't sound very romantic. They'd had a torrid night and then she'd cooled to him completely once he'd discovered her secret. She didn't seem to think that the news of her pregnancy should have affected him the way it did. Maybe he'd made too much of what he'd come to view as their relationship. Still, he couldn't just leave things this way.

He tried not to dwell on the fact that Rose still hadn't confirmed or denied the existence of another man. She'd just let things slide.

Maybe he should have, too. If only he wasn't so damnably drawn to her...

It had taken Aunt Beth's coaxing and finally coming up with tickets to this play before Rose deigned to say so much as a single word to him.

But she'd been worn down during the course of the day and he meant to keep working on her until she agreed to what he had to say. After all, it was in her best interests. He'd meant what he'd said to Beth. A woman just didn't go back to a place like Mission Creek and have herself a baby, then expect nothing else to change. Beth knew that as well as he did, even if she'd been away from Mission Creek all these years.

It didn't matter that Rose was Archy Wainwright's daughter. That only meant that people wouldn't say anything to her face, or where she could hear them. But they'd talk behind her back and that was a fact.

The very thought made Matt's blood boil. No one had the right to say disparaging things about Rose. Not while he could draw breath and do something about it.

The ring box and its contents was burning a hole in his pocket. He'd borrowed the engagement ring from Beth to visually support the statement of his intentions that he was about to make. Beth's second husband had given it to her when they'd gotten engaged, but she'd offered it to Matt permanently. When he'd declined, Beth had sworn that the ring held no sentimental value to her. She'd only kept it because "the stinker didn't want me to." After finding her husband of seven years in bed with a much younger woman, Beth had thought she'd earned not only the right to keep her jewelry after the divorce, but everything else she could get by hook or crook, as well.

He noted that Rose looked as if she was trying to locate a cab. It was too soon to go home, even if the hour was late.

"Would you like to get something to eat?"

Rose shook her head. "It's getting kind of late." And she needed her sleep for the baby as well as for herself.

"Some coffee, then?" His mind scrambled as he searched for a way to keep her out. Beth's suggestion about proposing in a public place was beginning to take on the guise of very solid advice. "You could have tea," he amended, suddenly remembering her condition.

His thoughtfulness got to her. Rose inclined her head.

"All right. There's a little coffee shop a block away. The Critic's Choice. It's where all the first-nighters congregate, waiting for the newspaper reviews to hit the streets."

He couldn't think of a more excruciating way to earn a living. Just worried about what Rose would say to him had him nervous, what was it like to worry about what strangers said? Strangers who could make or break your career with a well-placed line.

Of course, there was no comparison if he examined what was at stake. On the one hand, it was just a play, a performance. On the other, he was looking at the rest of his life.

At the rest of *their* lives, he thought, slanting a glance at Rose.

There was something in his look that she couldn't read. "What?"

He wasn't about to tell her what he was thinking. That would only scare her off. "Just noticing how pretty you look tonight."

Her hair was curling from the humidity, the light blue and white halter dress was beginning to stick to her even though she'd only just now been inside the air-conditioned theater. Humidity was descending rapidly.

She'd had better days—and nights. She shrugged off the compliment. "Must be the poor lighting," she muttered.

He stopped to place his hand beneath her chin, as if to examine her face from several angles. But it was her eyes he wanted to see. Her eyes, which at times were the only clue he had as to what was going on inside her head.

This wasn't one of those times.

"The lighting's just fine, Rose."

She didn't know why, but his assertion made her smile even more broadly.

The café had a lovely outdoor area that was surrounded by black wrought iron. Rose sat nursing her tall glass of herbal iced tea, watching the ice cubes melt. The waitress was backing away after bringing Matt another cup of coffee. It was close to midnight.

"That's your third cup," Rose noted. She set her glass back on the table. The condensation on the sides ran down to pool at the base of the glass where it met the table. "Is something wrong?"

Since he couldn't drink anything strong here, he was searching for a drop of courage in his coffee. He figured being wired might help him face her down until he got the answer that would do both of them the most amount of good.

"No, they just make great coffee."

"The best," she agreed. She'd come here on her first day in New York and had broken down to have a single cup of coffee herself. In deference to the new life she was carrying, she'd opted for a latte, heavy on the milk. The tea, she thought, playing with the straw, was almost as good. "But you have any more of that and we're going to have to tie a string to your ankle to keep you from flying away. I know how much caffeine is in that. You must be completely wired."

"Not completely." Matt set the cup down. No more coffee, no more excuses. It was time he got to the point of all this. "Rose, I want... I want... Oh, hell." He'd never been good with words, any words, no matter what the occasion. His heart and lips just weren't connected that way. He'd never minded it, until just now. "This says it all." He placed the ring box on the table.

Rose's eyes narrowed. She stopped bobbing ice chips with her straw. But she made no move to pick up the box to pull it toward her.

His impatience grew to almost unmanageable proportions. "Well, come on, aren't you going to open it?"

She recognized the box. Beth had shown it to her once. She'd offered to have the ring made over for her then, but Rose had declined.

"I don't have to open it. It's Aunt Beth's third engagement ring." There were two rings ahead of that one. There was the ring from her first husband, and one from someone named Hal, who'd died before they could get married. "Why do you want me to look at Aunt Beth's third engagement ring?"

"I don't want you to look at it. I want you to wear it."

That made it worse. "Why do you want me to wear Aunt Beth's third engagement ring?"

She made it sound like an open-ended series. "It's not Beth's. Technically, it's mine if I want it. She offered to give it to me."

Rose knew where Matt was going with this and she didn't want him to get there. "Congratulations. I hope the two of you are very happy together. I wish you both the best of luck."

"Damn it, Rose." He realized he'd raised his voice

and people at the nearby table were staring at him. Matt lowered his tone, though it took effort to keep it under control. She exasperated him faster than anyone ever had. "I don't want to get engaged to your aunt Beth. I'm trying to get engaged to you."

Damn it, he'd said it. Said what she'd wanted to hear. What she couldn't say yes to. "Then I suggest you get yourself another hobby, Matt, because this isn't going to happen."

Why was she being so damn stubborn about this? He had every right to be angry at her, yet she was acting as if this was somehow all his fault. "Rose, the baby needs a last name."

She pulled herself up. "It'll have a last name. It'll be a Wainwright."

"It can also be a Carson." He reached for her hand, but she pulled it away. "Damn it, Rose, I'm trying to protect you."

"Well, don't bother. I can protect myself."

"Like you did about this baby."

Hurt, angry, her eyes grew to small, angry slits. "That wasn't fair."

He realized his mistake the moment he'd said the words. "I didn't mean that."

"Didn't you?" Hurt, she had half a mind to hurl the ring, box and all at him, but it was Beth's, so she left it where it was. She blew out a breath. "I might have guessed you'd be a throwback."

Now what was she talking about? he asked himself. "What do you mean by that?"

"This is the twenty-first century." Not wanting to be the main floor show, Rose leaned over the table, her voice low, her anger barely suppressed. "Women have babies without husbands all the time. I'm not going to take your pity, or your guilt, or your inverted sense of what's right and wrong in this world. I can stand on my own without you or anyone else. Coming out here was proof of that."

It had taken courage to temporarily sever ties with the people she had always turned to in times of stress and unhappiness. She'd opted to shield them—and this big dumb jerk in front of her, as well.

She had to be crazy, she decided. There was no other explanation for it.

"You've got Aunt Beth," he pointed out. "That doesn't strike me as very independent."

She was almost at the breaking point. "Are you deliberately trying to pick a fight with me?"

"No, I'm deliberately trying to get engaged to you." He was asking her to marry him. What was so terrible about that? What was she so angry about? Didn't she realize what he was risking with this proposal? His family would be furious with him, yet he was risking their wrath for her. What more did the woman need? "Rose, I'm giving it my best shot."

He made it sound like some kind of test he had to

pass, some nebulous contest as in the *Odyssey*. Rose had enough.

She got up from the table. "All right, you gave it your best shot. And you missed the target. By a hell of a country mile. Now if you don't mind, I'm going to get a cab and go to my co-dependent home."

He had no idea what the hell she was babbling about, only that the streets were dangerous. "It's late."

"Beauty and brains, too. You are a catch," she said sarcastically. "For someone else, not me."

He caught her hand as she turned away. "Why? Why not you? You made love with me last night."

She flushed as a passing waiter glanced first at her, then at Matt and smiled his approval. "That didn't mean anything," she said.

"It felt like it meant something," Matt insisted.

It felt as if it had meant something to her, too, but she wasn't about to say that. It would give him too much leverage, and he had far too much as it was.

Abruptly pushing him away from her, she turned on her heel and hurried around the circumference of the wrought iron fence. Skirting a party of five that had picked this moment to come in, she made her way out the gate.

Quickly, she ran down the block. Suddenly drained, she looked around for a cab. She couldn't encourage Matt, couldn't let him do the honorable thing. Not just to give the baby a name. There had to be more to it than that, more to make a good marriage that would be facing so many obstacles. The only way she was ever going to say yes to him would be if he told her he loved her. Really loved her. Because with love, all things were possible.

But he was doing the "honorable" thing. She'd heard him say so as much to Beth. The word love hadn't entered into the conversation and she wasn't about to commit her soul to a man who didn't love her.

Caught off guard by her sudden escape, Matt quickly dug into his pocket and peeled out several bills to cover the drinks. Tossing the money onto the table, he debated following Rose's path, but that would put him behind. He needed to catch her before she could get a cab.

"Excuse me," he said to the person blocking his way. Physically moving the woman aside, Matt hopped over the fence.

Catching up to Rose in several strides, he grabbed her arm before she could get away again.

"What the hell's gotten into you?" he demanded.

She jerked her arm out of his grasp. "That's none of your business."

A cab pulled up almost at their feet. The driver stuck out his head. "He bothering you, ma'am?"

Matt cut her off before she had a chance to say anything or to get into the cab without him. "No, it's just a friendly misunderstanding. Thanks for asking, but no one's bothering her.''

But she was certainly bothering him, Matt thought, wrapping his hand around the ring box that was now back in his pocket.

Thirteen

She wanted to get away from him. Needed to get away from him.

Get away before she weakened and accepted the proposal for all the wrong reasons. Because there was part of her that was afraid to face having this baby alone. Because he *was* the baby's father and a baby should have his or her father close by. But most of all, because she didn't want to face each day of the rest of her life without him beside her.

But those were all cowardly reasons, driven by cowardly feelings, and she was a Wainwright. Wainwrights weren't cowards. She had her pride.

That and an enormous knot in her stomach.

Without warning, Rose suddenly yanked open the rear door of the cab and jumped in, slamming it behind her. She leaned forward in her seat.

"Fifty-ninth and Central Park West," she told the driver. "Quick."

"You got it."

But before the driver could step on the gas and peel away from the sidewalk in true getaway style, Matt opened the door and got into the cab with her. The driver's foot hit the brake again, rocking the vehicle. His Yankees cap pulled down low over his long, flowing gray hair, he twisted around in his seat.

He eyed Matt. "Lady, I ain't going anywhere unless you want me to."

Rose looked accusingly at Matt. But she knew he'd only find another cab and follow her back to Beth's apartment. After all, his clothes were still there. But not for long.

With effort, she let her anger abate. "It's all right."

"You sure?" the driver pressed. "He ain't holding a gun on you or nothing, is he?"

Matt was just about at the end of his patience, his temper threatening to erupt. "Look, fella, butt out. All I did was ask her to marry me."

The driver had turned back to the road. Hands poised on the wheel, the cabbie glanced at Matt in the rearview mirror. "Well, maybe she doesn't want to marry you. You ever think of that?"

Rose sighed and shook her head, moving over as far against the opposite door as possible. She looked at Matt and did what she thought she'd never do. She lied. "I don't."

The driver laughed under his breath. "Well, that settles it, don't it? No means no around here, buddy. You're outta luck."

Matt didn't need this. For two cents, he thought angrily, he'd get out of the cab and walk back to Beth's. Or all the way home to Texas. But then he'd be no better off than before and it would settle nothing.

Ignoring the annoying man in the front seat, Matt looked at her.

"Why not, Rose? You love me," he insisted. "I know you love me." He wasn't sure about many things in the world, but he was sure about that. The sun came up in the morning and Rose loved him. He could see it in her eyes, just like Beth had said. He could taste it in her kiss, feel it in the way she gave herself to him. In the way she took his heart.

"Hey, it's pretty clear that she doesn't," the cabbie retorted.

"Will you shut up and just drive?" Matt ordered, sending a scathing look the driver's way before he turned to her again. "Rose?"

He was telling her he knew she loved him. How pathetic did that make her seem? Rose thought. He knew, and yet he still made no mention of his own feelings for her. That made it crystal clear just what his feelings were. Nonexistent, except for some cock-eyed notion about honor.

She shifted until her body was facing his. She looked like a warrior about to go into battle.

"Oh, you know I love you, do you? Well, maybe he's right—" she pointed to the driver "—maybe I don't. Maybe it was just what I said it was—nothing more than a passing fling that we got caught up in."

Stopped at a red light, the driver craned his neck to look at them. "You tell 'im, girl."

Matt glared at the driver, his silent warning clear, then he looked back at Rose. "I didn't think you were that kind of a girl."

She was tired of being dictated to, tired of having other people think they knew what was best for her without asking. Even Aunt Beth was guilty of that. Indignant, she pulled herself up.

"Woman," she corrected heatedly. "I'm not a girl. I'm a woman, Matt, and maybe you don't know me at all."

Matt's mouth dropped open. He gestured toward the infuriating driver. "He just called you a girl and you didn't bite his head off."

She was breathing hard, her anger at a fever pitch. She was struggling to hold back tears. "He's not the one making assumptions."

The cab had stopped moving. "If anybody's interested, we're here," the driver announced.

Reaching into her purse, Rose pulled out a ten and held it out to the driver as she started to exit.

Another emasculating maneuver on her part, Matt thought. The woman was full of them. "Oh, no, you don't. You're not paying for me. I rode in this cab and I'm paying for it."

But Rose had already bolted, leaving the driver with the money.

The cabbie shook his head, looking at Matt with

something akin to pity in his eyes. "Mister, you've got a hell of a long way to go in figuring out what women want." Obligingly, the driver allowed him to change the first ten-dollar bill with a second. As if that somehow made a difference in the scheme of things. "You gotta sweet talk 'em if you want to get anywhere."

Now he was getting advice on his love life from a cabdriver who smelled of some strange exotic spice with every word he uttered. Matt wondered if he could sink any lower in this city.

"Thanks," Matt snapped over his shoulder coldly, hurrying out of the cab and after Rose.

He caught up to her within the building just as the elevator doors opened on the ground floor.

"Here's your money." He thrust the bill at her as an elderly couple got out of the elevator.

Rose nodded in greeting and entered the elevator. She jabbed the button for the twentieth floor, praying the doors would snap shut like a steel trap.

But Matt thrust his arm in and stopped the doors from closing. As they bounced back, he got in beside her.

For the moment, they were alone.

"Look, I've put up with insults and with a cabdriver who thinks he's Dear Abby. That's got to stand for something." He bit back his exasperation. "Now why won't you marry me?"

Why wouldn't he just accept her answer and back

off? Why was he making this so hard for her? If he didn't stop badgering her, she was going to give in and that would be disastrous for all of them—her, him and the baby that was to be.

"For openers," Rose retorted, "a marriage between a Carson and a Wainwright is doomed from the start, or have you forgotten that?"

"No, I haven't forgotten that, but I figure we'll handle it." The elevator stopped on the tenth floor. A couple was about to get in, but he put out his hand, stopping them. He pressed the button for the doors to close again. "Sorry, folks, private car. Another one'll be right along." He turned his attention back to Rose as if he'd never interrupted himself. "Just like we'll handle having this baby when he or she comes along."

She felt her stomach lurching as they arrived on Beth's floor. Rose didn't know if it was the baby protesting, or if Matt had gotten her so agitated that her stomach was churning.

"You're not handling anything because you don't figure into this." The doors opened and she stormed off the elevator without looking back.

Matt was right behind her. There was no way he was going to allow this argument to be over until he won. "The hell I don't."

Incensed, Rose stabbed the key into the lock, turning it until the door opened. Matt wasn't backing off and she needed reinforcements.

"Aunt Beth," she called loudly, looking around. "We're home." Her heart sank. There was no answer. Wasn't that woman ever home, she thought in exasperation. "Aunt Beth!" But there was still nothing.

Matt looked at her triumphantly. He knew what she was up to. "Looks like she's not here to help you."

"Help me?" Rose hated being transparent. "I don't need any help." She turned away from him.

Matt jumped in front of her. "Then why are you always running away?"

That got to her, as he'd known it would.

"I am *not* running away."

But he knew better. He indicated the apartment and what it represented. "What do you call this?"

Her eyes narrowed. Where did he get off challenging her this way? "Staying away from a crazy person. Can't you get it through your head? I never want to see you again."

The words slammed into him with the strength of a depth charge. He stood his ground and took it, then looked at her. "Do you mean that?"

"Yes." She couldn't bear the sadness she saw suddenly come into his eyes. "No." At her wit's end, Rose threw up her hands and turned away again. "I don't know what I mean."

That was all he needed to hear. Matt came up behind her, whispering against her hair. "You're too confused to make up your own mind. Let me make it up for you.''

She twisted around to face him and found herself looking up into his eyes. Scant inches away from his lips. The fight suddenly leeched out of her. ''Oh, you'd like that, wouldn't you?''

''Yes.'' His mouth was suddenly closer to her than her own thoughts. ''I would.''

It was, she realized, the beginning of the end.

The next moment Matt was kissing her. Kissing her utterly senseless. The moment his mouth came down on hers, all the pent-up emotions, the barely contained fire she was feeling inside, ignited, exploding within her.

She realized how futile it was for her to keep Matt at arm's length when all she really wanted was to enfold him in those same arms.

It was a mess, a royal mess, and she had no idea how to straighten things out.

Even when she'd said the words to send him away, she knew she was lying, knew when Matt pressed her about it that she just couldn't maintain the lie, not even for his own good.

More than anything, she didn't want him to go. She wanted him to stay. To stay and be her hero, her knight in shining armor.

Her baby's father.

With a sigh that echoed of pure surrender, Rose wound her arms around his neck and kissed him back for all she was worth, putting her soul into it, because her heart was already there.

Matt wanted to make love to her right here, in the foyer. But instead of undressing Rose the way he desperately yearned to, the way he had the first time they'd made love in Beth's apartment, Matt picked Rose up in his arms and started to walk down the hall.

Even as she settled into his arms, Rose looked at him, confused.

He couldn't resist pressing one kiss to her forehead. How had this happened? How had he lost his heart so completely when he wasn't looking?

"We don't know when Beth's coming back," he pointed out, "and I don't want her surprising us."

"Why?" Her mouth curved and he could swear she looked seductive and mischievous at the same time. "What are 'us' going to be doing?"

He shouldered open the door to her bedroom, then, still holding her, closed it with his back.

"Exactly what we want to be doing."

He set her down slowly, so that the length of her body slid along his, arousing him even more than he already was. Like a flash fire, desire flared in his veins.

"Baby, all I've thought about is making love with you. Night and day, day and night, looking at those silly paintings in the Metropolis—"

"Metropolitan Museum of Art," she corrected, unable to hold back her grin.

"Whatever. Even when you led me through all those dinosaur bones," he continued, "all I could think of was getting you alone and loving you."

"You mean making love with me."

He figured it was the librarian in her that caused Rose to correct him. But this time, she wasn't entirely right. "That, too."

She cocked her head, looking at him. "What do you mean, 'that, too'?"

He didn't want to talk, he wanted to make love with her. Until he couldn't drag a breath into his tired, used-up body.

"Woman, how many ways do you want me to spell it out to you?"

Now he had really lost her, although she knew what she wanted him to mean. But he probably didn't and Rose refused to allow herself to get carried away.

"The traditional way would be nice," she coaxed. "With your mouth."

He sighed, shaking his head. The woman required a great deal of patience. But in the long run, he knew she was worth it. Worth everything. "That's what I've been doing."

He leaned forward to kiss her, but she put her fingers to his lips, stopping him. "I meant words."

He backed off for a moment, his eyes searching her face. "Do you need them?"

She nodded her head solemnly. "Yes." Maybe it was weak of her, but she did. She needed to hear them said, at least once. She could only go so far on faith, on supposition.

"Then you've got them," he said with resignation. "I love you." Having said them, he said them again. And more. "I love you so much that it hurts to breathe sometimes." He caressed her face, cupped her cheek. Brought her mouth closer to his. "That it hurts to be in a room where you're not. That when I found out that you'd taken off, something inside of me felt like it was shriveling up and dying." He swallowed, having surprised even himself with the feeling behind his words. Slowly he released a breath, then asked, "There, are you satisfied?"

The corners of her mouth dimpled. "Almost."

"Almost?" he echoed. "Hell, woman, what's it going to take?"

On her toes, she wound her arms around his neck, her body tempting his. "Show me."

Matt laughed. This was more like it.

"That's what I've been trying to do all along," he said. Leaning over, he softly kissed her neck, sending such shock waves through her that she didn't realize he was undoing the knot at the back of her neck until the halter top sighed down to her waist.

Matt backed away just enough to look down at her nude breasts. He could feel himself fill with longing. With both hands cupping her, he continued kissing her mouth as if his very existence on earth depended on it.

He kissed her over and over again until they were both almost crazed with desire.

She wanted him. Nothing meant anything anymore. Not her excuses, not her own selfless act, nothing. It all faded away in the heat of her desire.

Her head was spinning again. Faster this time than the last. It was all she could do to keep herself grounded, if only just a little bit.

Fumbling, she found the belt at his waist and undid it. She needed to touch as much as she needed to be touched.

An urgency spilled through her limbs, her very core, as she tugged away the clothing that kept his body from hers.

Unbuttoning, unnotching, unzipping. Whatever it took to be closer to him.

And then there was nothing left between them, not even air.

In a tangle of entwined limbs, they fell onto the bed, their hands touching, caressing, teasing. By now they were far more familiar with each other's bodies, with each other's erogenous zones than they were with their own.

The excitement built nonetheless. Each knew what was there, awaiting them, but the anticipation of that thrill, that surging moment, only made it that much greater.

It was the promise of something different, but the pleasure of the same.

There was comfort in that. Joy in that. And a rush that waited to embrace them.

They worked their way toward it, each driving the other into a fever pitch. Each wanting to share that feeling, that elation.

She was determined to pleasure him the way he'd never been pleasured before. The fact that Matt was far more experienced in this world of quickening pulses, of erotic moments, didn't stop her. It made her only that much more determined.

Instincts, she told herself, counted for something. Her own body throbbing urgently, Rose pressed Matt down against the mattress, her hand hovering over him possessively.

When she curled her fingers around him, she saw the look of pure desire flash in his eyes. A secret, delicious feeling of empowerment came over her as she stroked the length of him, bringing him just a hairbreadth short of climax.

She surprised him. Though she'd been every inch a wild lover, far more than he had ever anticipated, she had never taken control like this before. She was driving him crazy.

Knowing that at any moment she would push him past the point of no return, he caught her by the shoulders, dragging her body up and over him. He shuddered as he barely held on by a thread.

"You're one hell of a wild woman," he told her, his voice throbbing with desire. "I didn't think they made women like you."

She leaned over him, her hair blanketing both sides of his face like a silken black curtain, her breasts moving tantalizingly along his chest.

"Think again."

Her eyes on his, mesmerizing him, Rose straddled him and began to move her hips slowly, driving him insane. Driving herself to the same destination.

Unable to hold back for long, she moved faster and faster, wanting to embrace the final crescendo she knew was waiting for her. For them.

She could feel the surge building, beginning in her loins and spreading out like rays of the sun to both ends of her body.

And then it came, the final summit, the final explosion.

The final descent.

Her heart beating as wildly as if she were free-falling, she groaned with ecstasy. She was just barely aware of his hands on her buttocks, squeezing as he made the same plunge with her.

The surge ricocheted through her, echoing madly until it finally began to fade away.

Exhausted, unable to even elicit a proper breath, Rose fell against Matt's damp chest, limp, spent and drained. She smiled, her mouth curving along his chest as she felt him gather her to him, holding her as if she was something elusive and precious.

Damn but she loved him. If she were to die this moment, it would be all right. Because the moment was perfect.

"Marry me, Rose," she heard him whisper against the top of her head. "Marry me and I swear I'll always be good to you. And I'll adopt the baby," he promised her, "and treat it as if it were my own."

The words echoed in her brain, fanning out to all parts of her. Compounding the guilt she was feeling.

The secret refused to remain inside her any longer. Rose picked up her head and looked at him. Common sense battled with her desire to tell the truth.

He had a right to know, she thought.

As she continued looking at him, she offered up a prayer for the wisdom not to make a mistake. She hadn't a clue as to whether her prayer was going to be answered.

All she knew was that she couldn't go on keeping this from Matt any longer. Her eyes locked with his.

"It's your baby."

Fourteen

Matt looked at her. It felt as if everything inside of him had frozen. Everything outside of him, as well.

"What did you say?"

His eyes had grown dark, unreadable. Rose felt a twinge of anxiety. The sentence was harder for her to say the second time than the first.

"It's your baby."

He heard the words, but they just weren't sinking in. It was as though they bounced off his mind like so many tiny beads.

"You're carrying my baby?" he asked incredulously.

Time and again from her father Rose had heard that the best defense was an offense. Besides, it was high time she took insult with the implication of Matt's words.

"Of course it's your baby," she said strongly, moving off him to his side. "There's never been anyone else but you. How *could* you think anything else?"

Matt sat up, astounded, confused. As the numbness within him receded, a host of emotions poured out like rampaging barbarian hordes attacking and pillaging a defenseless village.

"Then why didn't you tell me as soon as you knew?" he demanded.

They'd already been all through this. "I didn't tell you for the very reason I already said—because I didn't want to see you skinned alive and have your hide nailed to the barn door the way my father threatened to do to whoever it was who got me pregnant," she reminded him. "Believe me, he would have done a lot worse if he'd known it was a Carson."

Why was he making her explain this to him? Matt knew the circumstances as well as she did. This was why she'd held back when she'd first met him, to prevent something like this from happening.

And here it was, happening anyway.

"Our two families hate the sight of each other, Matt. And I have no intentions of letting you marry me so you can do the right thing and give the baby a name. I'm not some head of cattle you can just brand because it wandered into your corral, and neither is the baby. Don't you see? I don't want to be in a marriage that *has* to be, I want to be in a marriage that was *meant* to be."

There was the librarian coming out in her again, he thought, annoyance nibbling away at him. He wasn't in the mood for word games. Rose was always playing with words. "What's the difference?"

"Happiness."

Dragging the sheet around her, she rose to her knees.

His back to her, Matt bent to pick up his pants. Standing, he pulled them on. She placed her hand on his back to make him turn around.

"You're angry," she said.

He closed the snap at the top and tossed her a heated look from over his shoulder. "Damn right I'm angry."

Now it was her turn to be confused. She'd finally told him the truth, finally alleviated his fear that she'd been unfaithful to him. What more did he want?

"Why?"

He turned around to face her. "Because you lied to me."

"I didn't lie." She was very careful about that. "I just didn't tell you the baby was yours. There's a difference."

He blew out a breath, frustrated. "You're playing games."

She didn't believe in games, because games had winners and losers and she hated the idea of anyone losing.

"No, I was trying to do the right thing for all of us." And it hadn't gotten her anywhere but miserable. "What kind of a marriage would we have if you felt you were forced into it?"

He took hold of her shoulders. She felt so small,

so frail, as if he could break her between his hands if he wasn't careful.

"Now you listen to me. Nobody's ever forced me to do anything—except you when you forced me to break up with you. Looks like you're the only one who can make me jump through hoops."

The sadness she saw in his eyes went straight to her gut, twisting a knife there. "That was never my intention."

He shrugged, releasing her. His anger abated, he sat down beside her on the bed.

"Yeah, well, that's what happened, though. But no more. I'm my own man—always have been, always will be." He looked at her again, his voice growing in volume and confidence. "And I'm going to do what I want."

She nodded, her eyes never leaving his. "All right."

He smiled, confident that Rose knew what was coming next as well as he did. "And what I really want is to marry you."

Her heart leaped, thrilled that he was still adamant about it. This time the protest was only halfhearted. "But—"

"No buts about it." His eyes dipped down as he took in the way the sheet clung to her curves. "Unless it's your sweet butt lying next to mine."

The hell with worrying about everything else and everybody else. Maybe it was time to concentrate on snatching a bit of happiness for herself. With Matt. "Are you sure this is what you want?"

Taking her hand in his, he raised it to his lips and kissed it. He looked at her from beneath hooded, sexy eyes. "Never more sure of anything in my life."

The tingle was traveling all through her, surging down to her toes and up along the roots of her hair. "It's not going to be easy."

He shifted on the bed so that he could gather her to him.

"Hell, I knew the minute I saw you it wasn't going to be easy. The first time I had you in my arms, the earth stood still and everything else faded away. I kind of like it that way." He pretended to get serious, although he felt far from serious. At the very least, he felt like crowing. "Now, are you going to say yes, or do I have to tie you up and kidnap you to a place where what you say won't matter."

"You'd do that?"

What she had to say would always matter to him, but for now he refrained from telling her that. What he did was open up his heart instead. "I'd do any-thing to have you in my life."

Her mouth curved. "They put people in jail for things like that these days."

She was referring to stalkers. What he felt didn't come with a label. And her happiness always came before his own. If he felt that she was truly happier without him than with him, as much as it would hurt, he'd walk away and leave her. But that, too, he kept to himself.

"It'd be worth it. But just so you know, no place is going to hold me. Not if it means keeping me away from you."

This time she grinned. Broadly. "Then I guess I have no choice."

He shook his head. "Nope, none." And then his eyes softened. "But it'd be nice to know that this was your choice."

"Would it matter?" She held her breath, waiting to hear his answer.

He couldn't do anything but tell her the truth. "It matters. Anything you think would matter." He poured out his heart in hopes that it would make her understand. "The two weeks I spent apart from you were the two longest weeks of my life. They felt like two years. A man can't endure that kind of thing on a regular basis." He pulled her to him. "So what do you say?"

She lifted her chin, answering his question with one of her own. "And you love me?"

"I already told you that."

She moved her body against his seductively. "Tell me again," she coaxed.

He could feel his voice hitching. "I love you. Satisfied?"

She sighed, threading her arms around his neck and

sitting back on her heels. "Only if you tell me that every morning of every day we're together."

His arm around her waist, Matt pulled her closer still. "You ask a hell of a lot, don't you? Those are your terms?"

She bobbed her head, the finality a given. "Those are my terms."

"Well, if I have no choice…you've got yourself a deal."

Matt lightly touched his lips to hers, then slowly deepened the kiss until it was large enough for both of them to get lost in. As he wrapped his arms around Rose, he lightly tugged away the sheet she'd tucked around herself.

She kissed him as if there was no tomorrow, had been no yesterday. As if there was nothing but the moment they were in, and it was both endless and fleeting, demanding that they make the most of it before it was gone.

It took Matt several seconds to realize what was going on. Holding on to her arms, he wedged a small space between them, then looked at her face. Her cheeks were damp.

"You're crying."

"No, I'm not…" It was a normal response to deny what her father viewed as an expression of weakness. "Maybe just a little," she allowed.

"Why?" His eyes swept over her. "Are you hurt? Is something wrong?"

Rose shook her head. "No, nothing's wrong and for the first time since I realized I was pregnant, I don't hurt." It was a time for truth-telling. "I'm crying because I'm so happy."

That was completely beyond him. Tears were for pain. He merely shook his head. "I am never going to understand women."

"There aren't going to *be* any women for you to understand, cowboy," she warned Matt playfully. "Only me."

He was grinning as he lowered his mouth to hers. "Sounds good to me."

Rose gladly gave herself up to the feeling that seized her in its grasp. And to the only man she had ever loved.

Exhausted beyond words, happier than he could recall ever being, Matt slowly shifted his weight until he was lying beside Rose. It amazed him that they'd actually wound up making love two more times. No doubt about it, the woman brought out a side to him he'd never even known existed.

"You sure this won't hurt the baby?"

She couldn't remember ever being this tired and this happy at the same time. The sensitivity he was displaying made her love him all the more.

"I guarantee the baby's smiling right now because its mommy is so happy."

"So I take it you haven't changed your mind?" It

had been several hours since he'd proposed and she'd accepted. When it came to Rose, he wasn't about to take things for granted anymore.

"No." And then a thought occurred to her. She shifted her head toward him. "Have you?"

"Not a chance." He ran his fingers along her cheek. "The sooner the better."

Out of nowhere, excitement suddenly ricocheted through her. Rose raised herself up on her elbow to look at him. "Let's go tell Aunt Beth."

Matt glanced over her head at the clock on the nightstand. "Rose, it's seven o'clock in the morning. Your aunt doesn't exactly keep regular hours. Let her sleep. We can tell her later."

Besides, he thought, his exhaustion was fading and he could feel desire stirring within him again. All he wanted to do was to stay in bed with Rose.

But Rose was already sitting up and looking around for her clothes. She saw Matt's pants lying on the floor instead.

"Aunt Beth will want to know, trust me. She's been singing your praises and telling me how wonderful you are ever since you got here."

Matt grinned, nodding. "The woman does have excellent taste, no arguing with that."

Rose laughed, throwing his pants at his head. "Yeah, well, don't forget to get dressed. We don't want to give Aunt Beth a heart attack."

He looked at Rose, surprised. "Heart attack?"

Maybe she didn't know her aunt as well as he thought she did. Until he'd come into her life, he knew Rose had been rather shy and sheltered. "Something tells me your aunt would take the sight of a naked man right in stride. I heard her talking about being in Woodstock during that big, blowout concert they had up there back in sixty-nine. Did you know she danced nude in the rain?"

"No, but that doesn't surprise me." She'd seen pictures of her aunt when she'd been younger. Still very attractive, the woman had been drop-dead gorgeous in her twenties. "Nothing about Aunt Beth surprises me. She likes to live every second of life." Rose debated getting completely dressed, then opted to just slip on her silk robe instead. She was too excited to wait any longer. "Ready?"

Matt glanced back at the bed. "I can't talk you out of this?"

Grabbing his hand, she began to tug him out of bed. She shook her head in response to his question. "If I don't tell someone, I'm going to explode and she's the only one who'd be happy for us."

He sighed, resigned. Throwing the covers off with his free hand, he got out of bed and grabbed his pants. "Okay, then, give me a minute."

Rose tried not to stare at him as he got dressed, desire flaring up within her all over again. It felt as if she was never going to get her fill of Matt. She sincerely prayed that day would never come.

She pretended to look at her watch, amusement dancing in her eyes. "I'll give you thirty seconds."

He was ready in twenty-nine. Still barefoot, he took her hand and walked out of the room.

"I still think this'll keep until later." They made the short trip from Rose's bedroom to Beth's. He nodded at the older woman's door. "You do the honors."

The wide grin on her lips threatened to go from ear to ear and split her face in two as she knocked on Beth's door. Her hand tightened on Matt's.

"Aunt Beth? I know it's early, but I—we," she amended, beaming at Matt, "have to talk to you."

There was the sound of shuffling and sudden movement behind the closed door. And then the thud. Rose and Matt exchanged glances.

"Did she fall out of bed?" Matt whispered to Rose. And then he tugged slightly on her hand. "Maybe we should come back later."

But Rose was determined. "No, that's okay. She's got to be up now. Aunt Beth, it's us, Rose and Matt. May we come in?"

"Rose *and* Matt?" Deep and husky, Beth's voice registered surprise from behind the door. There was more shuffling, and then she urged, "Come in, come in."

Excited, Rose opened the door, then stopped short as her mouth dropped open. Beth was not alone. In bed beside her was a hauntingly handsome young man Rose vaguely recognized as one of the acting students that her aunt taught. If she had to guess, she would have said that he was about thirty years old. Aunt Beth hadn't seen thirty—other than her lover—in quite some time.

Making herself more comfortable against her pillows, Beth tucked the sheet more securely around her ample breasts.

"Oh, don't look so shocked, Rose. You'd think you were the parent and I was the child." Her smile spread to take in Matt. "Remember, my dears, life is to be savored, every last bite." She turned toward the young man beside her who looked incredibly at ease, given the situation. "I think you know Bryce."

"Your student," Rose concluded, for the moment forgetting all about what had brought her into Beth's room in the first place. She knew all the stories about Beth's wild and so-called wicked youth, but she'd just assumed that it was all behind her. If she thought of Beth being in the company of men, she naturally assumed that they would be closer to her aunt's age, not her own.

Beth held up a finger. "Former student, actually. Bryce officially last took my class over a year ago." She turned toward him. "Didn't you, dear?"

"But I saw him here the other night," Rose protested. "With the others."

Beth waved away the protest and the worry line she saw forming across Rose's forehead. No matter what she said, the girl was very much Archy's daughter, Beth thought.

"That's unofficial. He graduated last June, but found that I had a profound influence on him." Beth patted Bryce's hand. "Wasn't that the way you worded it, dear?"

"Profound," Bryce agreed. It was obvious that he thought of Beth as more than his match and was as comfortable with the arrangement as Rose was uncomfortable. He looked at Matt. "Your aunt's the youngest woman I know." Bryce's look shifted to Rose. "No offense."

"None taken," she murmured.

Rose felt a laugh bubbling within her throat. Why shouldn't Beth have someone in her life? From everything she'd learned about her aunt and seen first-hand since she'd arrived, Bryce probably had trouble keeping up with the woman.

This was wonderful. Her life was finally in order. Matt was going to stick by her, not because he had to but because he wanted to. She'd finally found someone to love her and to love back, and it appeared that Beth had done the same, too.

Like Queen Victoria holding court in her bedchamber, Beth made herself comfortable against the headboard. She smiled benevolently at the young couple in front of her.

"So I take it you've both come to your senses and decided to stop all this foolish behavior. Am I right?"

She didn't wait for an answer; she could tell by the looks on their faces. "It's about time." Beth looked from one to the other. "There's more?"

Rose nodded, pressing her lips together to rein in her exuberance. She wanted to shout the announcement from the top of the tallest building in New York. Beth's bedroom was going to have to do.

"We're getting married."

"Hallelujah!" Beth clapped her hands together enthusiastically. "This calls for a celebration. Matt, be a dear and hand me my robe." She extended her hand, indicating the electric-blue kimono on the back of her vanity chair. "Can't exactly pour champagne au naturel now, can we?"

Rose had no trouble visualizing that and knew it was something that her aunt was more than capable of. Before Matt could reach for the robe, Rose got it for her. Then she hooked her arm through Matt's and turned him toward the opposite wall as Beth donned the robe.

The woman, Matt thought, was clearly a pistol. He grinned and whispered to Rose, "Maybe we can persuade your aunt to come to Mission Creek for a visit. I'm sure your father would love having her and Bryce around for a few weeks."

That would certainly bring out the fireworks, Rose thought. She knew exactly how her father would react to her aunt arriving with a man young enough to be her son. Archy Wainwright had been born old and judgmental.

Rose grinned. "It'd certainly take the heat off the two of us for a while."

Oblivious to where he was, aware only of her, Matt slipped his arms around Rose, nuzzling her. "I *never* want the heat off us."

Coming up behind them, Beth placed a hand on each of their shoulders. "So, shall we go look for that special bottle of champagne, dears?"

Rose turned around and looked at her aunt quizzically. "Special bottle?"

"Yes. I have a rare old bottle I've been saving for an occasion such as this." Leading the procession, Beth swept out of her bedroom. "I put it on ice the evening you turned up on our doorstep, Matthew."

Mystified, Matt asked, "Why?"

She spared him a knowing glance. "Because I knew that this was going to have a happy ending. The Carson boys are nothing if not determined."

Stubborn jackasses was the way her father described them, Rose thought. But her aunt sounded as if she was speaking from firsthand knowledge.

Rose looked at her aunt. "How would you know?"

Beth inclined her head, her eyes indicating the young man who was bringing up the rear. "Now is not the time to go into details, my dear. I'll save that story for another time," she promised, then raised her voice. "Come along, Bryce. You can make the toast."

Obligingly, Bryce moved up to the head of the line beside Beth. Rose caught a whiff of cologne as he passed her and it jarred something in the back of her mind. Her eyes widened as she remembered the mugger near the Metropolitan Museum of Art. Her mouth fell open as her eyes shifted from Bryce and met Beth's.

Very slowly, Beth smiled.

Rose could only shake her head.

"To the kitchen, shall we?" Beth urged.

But as they were about to enter, the doorbell rang.

"Who could that be at this hour?" Rose asked.

Brightening, Beth changed direction and headed for the front door. "That's what I love about New Yorkers. They really do never sleep." She raised her voice. "Who is it?"

"Justin Wainwright, Aunt Beth," the deep male voice on the other side of the door announced. "I've come for Rose."

Fifteen

Rose stared at Matt, wide-eyed and stunned. "What is my brother doing here?"

Though there was no way he could have heard her, the answer to her question came through the door. "Let me in, Aunt Beth. I heard that Matt Carson was looking for her."

Beth silently indicated to Bryce to usher Matt and Rose out onto the terrace and to close the curtains. While he did that, she stalled for time.

"Why would he do that?" she asked through the door.

"C'mon, Aunt Beth, just open the door and let me in."

Beth glanced back toward Bryce, who nodded. With the prey safely hidden, she opened the door and threw her arms around her nephew in an enthusiastic embrace.

"Justin, it's been far too long. C'mon, give your aunt a little love."

Dutifully, he hugged her, though clearly it was awkward for him. Like his father, Justin, Beth knew, wasn't given to demonstrative affection.

Justin stepped back and around. "Is Rose asleep?" He started toward the rear of the apartment.

"No, Rose isn't asleep. Rose is gone," Beth informed him innocently.

Justin pivoted back on his heel. Though there was a stubborn core to Rose, his sister wasn't given to adventures. She wouldn't have just taken off like that.

"Rose is gone?" he echoed. "What do you mean? It's seven in the morning. Why isn't she in her bed?"

He strode down the hallway, opening doors.

Beth followed his progress with a growing anxiety she did her best to hide. She sincerely hoped that the two people on the balcony would connect the dots and figure out that she'd had Bryce place them there because of the immediate proximity to her neighbor's balcony. There was a small common wall that could easily be climbed. The Van Holdens were in Europe. She'd mentioned that just yesterday and now hoped one of them remembered.

"What the hell is this?" Justin's voice boomed when he took in the scene in Rose's room. The bed was a tangled heap of linens and pillows, while the floor was littered with discarded clothing—Rose's and a man's shirt.

Justin picked up the shirt with his fingertips. He held it aloft as if it were Exhibit A in a crime scene investigation. He looked at Beth.

"Now, Justin, Rose is a grown woman. Don't you think she's got a right to come and go as she pleases with whomever she pleases without first checking in and running it by me?''

Disgusted, Justin tossed the shirt onto the bed. His face was dour as he said, ''The last time she came and went as she pleased, she got herself in the family way. And talk is the baby belongs to that Carson bastard.''

The conversation had an incredible feel of déjà vu for Beth. She was suddenly in her father's house, listening to both her father and her brother Archy rave, airing their disapproval of the man she was seeing at the time, a wonderfully gifted Native American who didn't meet their standards.

She took umbrage for Matt just as the doorbell rang again. She waved Bryce off to the door.

''Be a dear, Bryce,'' she requested, then turned to look at her nephew. ''Matt Carson isn't a bastard, he's a perfectly nice young man.'' Justin looked at her in astonishment. She fisted her hands at her waist. Nothing made her angrier than unwarranted prejudice. ''Something you would find out if you ever sat down and talked to him.''

''Then he has been here?'' Justin demanded.

''Where's my brother?''

At the sound of another angry voice, Beth and Justin turned to see Flynt Carson striding into the room. The latter spared a frosty glance and nod toward the young man, then took off his hat as he looked at Beth.

"Where's my brother?" he repeated, tagging on a "ma'am," to the end of his inquiry.

It wasn't hard for Beth to figure out who this one belonged to. He had Matt's bone structure. If she wasn't careful, she was going to have an old-fashioned free-for-all right here in her apartment.

Beth placed a hand to her breast, looking toward Bryce. "Oh, my. If I knew I was going to have so many visitors, I would have arranged to have breakfast sent in." Still stalling for time, she pretended not to know her latest visitor. "And you are?"

"Flynt Carson, ma'am. I've come looking for my little brother, Matt. Word has it that he's here."

Beth spread her hands wide, the sleeves of her kimono all but dragging on the floor. "I'm afraid not. As I was telling my nephew, there's no one inside this apartment but Bryce, you boys and me." She punctuated her declaration with an innocent look.

Justin scowled. "Then exactly where is Rose? C'mon, Aunt Beth, you've got to know."

"Where's Matt?" Flynt pressed. Shouted, the questions overlapped one another.

With a sigh, Beth pretended to think. And then her eyes brightened as if the idea had just occurred to her. "You might try city hall."

"City hall?" Flynt demanded. It was half question, half gasp. When he'd told Matt to stop moping around and go after the woman who'd dumped him, he'd had no idea that he was telling him to go after a Wainwright. Damn it, why didn't the kid tell him? He would have never sent his brother after her if he'd known. Matt was always too closemouthed for anyone's good.

"Yes," Beth said, happy the thought had come to her. It was going to be the quickest way to get the men out of her apartment. She gave the duo a significant look. "And you might just think about calling each other brother-in-law."

The responses were quick and to the point.

"The hell we will."

"Not in a million years."

Beth folded her hands serenely, burying them beneath the sleeves of her kimono.

"I'd suggest that you boys seriously rethink those sentiments. There's a baby on the way that's part Wainwright, part Carson. Can't play tug-of-war with a baby. I'd say that baby is the best argument for mending that fence, or burying that hatchet or whatever silly metaphor you want to use for finally making things right between all of you again."

Her lecture at an end, Beth looked expectantly from one handsome face to the other. What she'd told them she meant from the bottom of her heart, but after more than her share of husbands and lovers, she knew the way a man's mind worked. Say "black," the response almost always will be "white." At this point, she just wanted them to leave so she could retrieve the lovebirds from wherever they had flown.

Justin looked at Flynt, hope suddenly flashing through his veins. He clung to it. ''Maybe they're not married yet.''

The thought sparked the two men into action and they turned as one toward the door.

''See you boys at Christmas,'' Beth called after them as they hurried away.

Bryce walked up behind Beth and slipped his arms around her waist. He nuzzled against her. ''When do you think they'll figure out that city hall isn't open yet?''

Beth laughed. ''Hopefully not before they're half-way downtown.''

The sound of raised voices coming from inside the apartment had increased. Matt recognized the new one first.

''That's my brother,'' he whispered to Rose. This couldn't be happening, he thought. ''What the hell is Flynt doing here?''

''Probably looking for you,'' Rose said. ''Hoping to stop you from making a horrible mistake.''

He didn't want her talking like that, or thinking like that. Matt took her into his arms. ''The only mistake I ever made was letting you go in the first place. I should have stood my ground and followed my heart.''

The voices were getting angrier. She knew what

her brother's temper was like when he was finally pushed to the limit. Not a pretty sight.

She indicated the wall. "Right now, I suggest we follow the yellow brick road before one of us winds up getting tarred and feathered."

He pressed a kiss to the top of her head. "I wouldn't let anything happen to you. Besides, I can handle my brother."

"I was thinking of mine. He takes after my father when it comes to being reasonable."

That said it all for Matt. "Then let's not give him a chance to catch us."

After climbing over the common wall, Matt picked up Rose and lifted her over to the other side. He grabbed her hand and crossed to the terrace door.

He tugged on it. It was locked.

Rose bit her lower lip. "I think Aunt Beth said they were away on a trip. Now what?"

"Now we see if my bad boy days paid off." He looked around for something small to use, then remembered the paper clip he had in his wallet. He'd put it on some scraps of business papers he wanted to hold together. Taking his wallet out, he pulled off the clip and straightened it to use on the lock.

After several moments the lock clicked and the door gave.

Rose could only shake her head. "You are a constant source of surprise to me."

"Always a good thing in a marriage," he assured her.

Slipping into the darkened living room, he closed the door behind them as silently as he could. "Sure hope your aunt's right about the people being away on vacation," he whispered against Rose's ear.

"I think she said they were going to Europe. I think it's a safe bet that they won't be back in the next ten minutes."

"Europe, huh?" His eyes slid over her as he suddenly recalled what she had on under her robe. "Well, then, what I've got in mind is going to take more than ten minutes."

Her eyes widened, but her smile was pure seduction. "But our brothers are next door."

He was already undoing the sash at her waist. "We won't ask them in."

A thrill went over her as the sash came undone and her robe parted invitingly. "Matt, this is positively decadent."

He was already coaxing the robe from her bare shoulders, kissing each as it became denuded. "It'll make a nice story to tell little whose-it-what's-it when he or she finally gets here."

"You can't tell stories like that to our child." She couldn't resist him any longer. "What will she think of us?"

Matt laughed against her hair, his hands caressing her, making her crazy. "He'll think that maybe his parents aren't the stick-in-the-muds all kids think their parents are.''

"She."

"He." He nipped her mouth. "Hell, we'll get one of each."

She was having trouble concentrating. "Doesn't always happen that way."

He pressed a ring of small, flowering kisses along her jawline, working his way to her neck. "We'll keep working at it until it does."

"Is this your way of keeping me barefoot and pregnant?" she asked thickly.

"Nope." The robe floated to the floor as he embraced her. "Just naked."

Rising up on her toes, she brought her mouth to his. "Sounds good to me.

Epilogue

At 10:00 a.m., it was too early for the lunch crowd. Except for Daisy at the bar, they were alone in the restaurant.

Matt reached for Rose's hand. It was ice cold. He wrapped his fingers around it. She was nervous. He wasn't exactly feeling calm himself, but he knew now wasn't the time to let her see that. This was the first hurdle they were facing together as husband and wife.

Taking a breath discreetly, Matt squeezed her hand. Rose looked at him. "It's going to be all right," he promised.

She nodded. She wanted to believe that, *had* to believe that. Otherwise, it was going to be just him and her. The two of them against the world.

The three of them, she amended, thinking of her baby. *Their* baby.

She'd always been so family oriented, the thought of a schism between her and her family was almost too much to bear. Rose was banking on their love for her to somehow engineer a truce between the two sides.

The late-morning sun found its way to the plain gold band on her left hand, highlighting it. Mrs. Matthew Carson. It was official. She belonged to him now. And he to her.

They'd gotten married at the altar in St. Patrick's Cathedral rather than at city hall the way they'd first decided. As always, bless her, Aunt Beth had known someone who could help. This time, it was a priest connected to the cathedral. Father Thomas Gannon had ushered them in after ten o'clock at night just a scant thirty-six hours ago. It was he who had performed the ceremony in front of God, Aunt Beth and their would-be mugger, Bryce.

Rose couldn't have asked for anything more perfect than the regal stained glass, the fine statues and the reverent hush within the old cathedral. She would have been satisfied marrying Matt under the stars on the prairie with words uttered by a justice of the peace, but it, she had to admit, had been as perfect as she could have envisioned.

Except, perhaps, to have had her family there.

But that was what today was all about. She and Matt had separately summoned their respective families to meet them at the temporary Men's Grill in the Lone Star Country Club.

She only prayed that fireworks wouldn't result as the various members of their two families ran into each other when they arrived at the club.

Her stomach suddenly tightened. She couldn't

make out the words, but she could hear her father's gruff voice just outside the door.

"Here they come," she said to Matt.

The door of the restaurant suddenly opened and Archy Wainwright strode in, followed closely by Ford Carson. Various members of both families spilled into the room, surprised, mystified and wary. Rather than mingle, each gravitated to a side, not quite sure what was going on.

Like a bullet, Archy made for his daughter.

"What the hell's the meaning of all this, Rose?" he demanded. "You're supposed to be in New York with that flaky sister of mine." Out of the corner of his eye, he caught a reproving look from his ex-wife, Kate, and tempered his tone.

As far as Rose knew, neither her brother nor Matt's had returned from New York yet. But it was the head of each family that she was concerned with now.

She took a deep breath and held on to Matt's hand more tightly.

"Matt and I have an announcement to make." Rose congratulated herself that her voice hadn't quavered in the face of her father's angry scowl.

Ford Carson's eyes narrowed. "What kind of announcement?" He turned to his son. "Is she doing the talkin' for you these days, boy?"

Matt squared his shoulders. He was used to his father's blunt way of speaking and pretty much immune to it. But he didn't want anything to hurt Rose. She'd been through enough as it was.

"I don't mind my wife taking the lead once in a while."

The room went deadly silent, shrouded in disbelief. The two sides regarded each other with uncomfortable wariness.

"Your what?" Ford thundered.

Archy glared accusingly at his daughter. "Is he the one who's responsible?"

Rose lifted her chin. "If you mean responsible for making me happy, Dad, then yes, Matt's the one who's responsible."

"Don't play your word games with me, girl." He pointed a short, stubby finger in Matt's direction. "Is he the one who forced himself on you?"

Matt moved forward, about to defend himself, but Rose thrust her arm in front of him to hold him in place. The last thing she wanted was for the two men who meant the most to her to get into it right in front of her.

"Nobody forced anything, Dad. I love Matt Carson and he loves me." She looked at Matt's father. "And yes, Mr. Carson, there is a baby on the way. A baby who's going to be half Carson, half Wainwright and who's going to need all of your love."

"Now, does the baby get it?" Matt wanted to know, looking from his father to Rose's. "Or do we tell him that his grandfathers are stubborn old men who let pride and a stupid, ancient feud get in the way of the best thing that's happened to their families in a long, long time? The choice is yours."

Both men stood regarding one another and the situation in complete silence, searching for a way not to rend their families asunder any further while still saving face.

Archy spoke first. He looked at his daughter, love winning out over pride. "Married, huh?"

She nodded her head and held up her hand with the ring on it. "Married."

He lifted his shoulder and let it drop in dismissive apathy. "Well, it don't count if it happened in a place like New York City."

She wasn't going to be outbullied by her father. Not this time. Rose looked at him pugnaciously. "It counts."

"No," Archy insisted. "It don't. Gotta do it up right." He slanted a look toward Ford, daring the man to disagree with him. "Texas style if this marriage is going to have a chance."

He took a step forward as he saw Ford approach Rose, but his ex-wife placed a restraining hand on his arm.

After a moment's hesitation, Ford embraced his son's new wife. When he released her, he echoed Archy's words, surprising everyone.

"That's my grandchild you're carrying and his parents are going to get married right."

"Don't be telling my daughter what to do," Archy warned darkly. Then his brow cleared slightly as he looked at Rose. "But for once in his life, Ford Carson's right. If this marriage is going to take, you've got to have the wedding out here." Grudgingly, he looked at Ford. Maybe it *was* time to put the past to rest. "At the place our grandfathers put together before things went sour."

Presenting himself in front of Ford, Archy huffed, frowning. "I guess I'm willing to give a truce a chance, for the sake of the kids, if you are." He put out his hand.

Ford stood regarding the hand that was being offered him. After a beat, he took it in his own callused one. "Never let it be said that a Wainwright's a bigger man than a Carson—" His eyes washed over Archy's less than trim waistline. "Unless they're talking about weight, of course."

Rose felt tears filling her eyes as she threw her arms around her father's neck. "Thank you, Dad."

He stroked her head. "Anything for my little girl," he said softly. Clearing his throat, he looked at Ford, who was embracing his own son in solemn congratulations. "Maybe it's high time we called an end to this feud, anyway."

Everyone in the room agreed with relief.

In another state, Dylan Bridges was dictating last-minute notes into his micro-recorder as he tossed clothes with his free hand into the suitcase that laid open on his bed.

There were myriad things to keep him here. In actuality, he had no time to spare. But time was the main factor now. He couldn't seem to shake the sense of urgency that had overtaken and haunted him since his father's telephone call.

He had a feeling that if he didn't go to see the judge, he would regret it for the rest of his life. Stopping his tape recorder, he reached for the portable telephone and punched in the number for the local airport.

"Hello? Yes, I'd like a ticket to Mission Creek, Texas. What? One way—for now."

* * * * *

Don't miss the next story from
Silhouette's
LONE STAR COUNTRY CLUB:

THE REBEL'S RETURN
by Beverly Barton
Available August 2002

*Turn the page for an excerpt from this
exciting romance…!*

One

Dylan Bridges removed his coat and tie, tossed them on the bed, then slipped out of his Italian loafers and padded across the lush carpet to the closet. He removed a pair of faded jeans from a wooden hanger and retrieved a Texas A&M T-shirt from the top drawer of a built-in dresser.

As he changed clothes, he chuckled, thinking about how surprised the good folks in his old hometown of Mission Creek would be if they could see him now. Seventeen years ago he'd been shipped off to the Texas Reform Center for Boys in Amarillo, and when he'd walked out of that place after serving his full two years, the last place on earth he'd wanted to go was back to Mission Creek. And the last person he'd wanted to see was his father. Yeah, his feelings for his old man had only grown more hostile during his incarceration. And even a sweet little letter from Maddie Delarue while he was serving time hadn't lessened his resentment toward her.

Dear Dylan,
I wanted to tell you how sorry I am that you were sent away to reform school. I know I

should have tried to help you in some way, but at the time I didn't have the courage to speak to my father on your behalf. Please know that I think about you. Stay strong and keep out of trouble while you're there. I've learned the hard way that life isn't always fair and can throw you some cruel punches.

If you want to write to me, send your letter to the post office box on the outside of the envelope.

Maddie

Figuring that she'd written the letter either as some do-good philanthropic club project or simply because she had a guilty conscience, Dylan hadn't responded. And he never received another letter from her. But truth be told, he'd never forgotten Maddie Delarue. In a totally illogical way, she remained the ultimate, unattainable goal.

Dylan made his way into the living room of his luxury penthouse apartment, poured himself a drink—Jack Daniel's, straight—and relaxed in the over-stuffed, tan-leather easy chair. Why was he thinking about Maddie, a girl he hadn't seen since he was sixteen? It wasn't as if he'd been pining away for her all these years. He hadn't. In his twenties women had come in and out of his life like tourists through a revolving door at a New York hotel. And now, at thirty-three and the wealthiest stockbroker in Dallas, all he had to do was snap his fingers and the lovely ladies came running.

The only reason he'd thought about Maddie was thanks to his plan to return to Mission Creek this week. He was going to do something he'd thought he would never do—go home to see his father. And, who knew? He'd probably run into Maddie while he was there. Maybe he'd make a point of it. Nothing would please him more than to show her—and everybody in Mission Creek—that the town bad boy had turned out all right.

The kid who'd been sent to reform school for stealing another man's Porsche now owned a Porsche of his own. And a Jag and several antique vehicles. His penthouse apartment had cost him in the millions; he owned a home in Aspen; and he was part owner of a chain of resort hotels in the Bahamas.

Oh, yeah, a part of him would love to rub Maddie Delarue's nose in his success. Of all the people back home, she was the only one he really wanted to impress. She was probably married now, with a couple of kids.

Since her father's death a few years ago, she was now the richest woman in Texas. Dylan chuckled. Hell, maybe she wouldn't be that impressed with him, after all.

Grinning, Dylan sipped on his whisky. Even after several days of mulling over the entire matter, he still found it difficult to believe that his father had called him. Out of the blue, after all this time, Judge Carl Bridges had set aside his unswerving pride and telephoned his only child.

"Son, I'm asking you to forgive me," Carl had said. "Can you find it in your heart to give your father a second chance? Is there any hope that we can put the past behind us and build a new relationship?"

Strange that he hadn't vented years of frustration and rage directly at his father. Even stranger was the fact that he, too, wanted nothing more than to put the past to rest, to reach out and forge a new relationship with his father. If staunch, unyielding Carl Bridges could admit mistakes and ask for forgiveness, then so could his son.

Dylan had ended his conversation with his father by saying, "Yeah, Dad, I'll think about coming to Mission Creek for a visit. I just need some time to get used to the idea."

This morning when he awoke, he decided right then, even before his first cup of coffee, that there was no better time than the present to find out if his dad and he could reconnect as father and son. Besides, he needed a vacation. He worked too much; even his closest friends told him he'd become a workaholic. But despite his wealth and great success, he didn't have anything else in his life that truly mattered. Only work. Long ago, he'd come to the conclusion that a guy couldn't count on anyone or anything except himself. Family was a bogus term. He felt as if he'd lost his only family when his mother died. The desire to marry and start a family of his own had eluded him, mainly because he'd never met a woman he thought he could spend the rest of his life with—never loved or trusted a woman enough to make a serious commitment.

He supposed he should call his father to apprise him of his plans, but he liked the idea of just showing up on his dad's doorstep and surprising him. He'd already chartered a private plane to fly him to Mission Ridge, the nearest airport to his hometown. He'd be home in time for supper. Maybe he'd take his dad to the country club, to the Empire Room. Now, wouldn't that be something—to go back to the Lone Star Country Club as a guest instead of an employee.

And who knew, maybe if things worked out with his father, he might even relocate to Mission Creek.

Escape to a place where a kiss is still a kiss...
Feel the breathless connection...
Fall in love as though it were
the very first time...
Experience the power of love!

Come to where favorite authors—such as
Diana Palmer, Stella Bagwell,
Marie Ferrarella and many more—
deliver heart-warming romance and genuine
emotion, time after time after time....

Silhouette Romance—
stories straight from the heart!

Where love comes alive™

passionate powerful provocative love stories that fulfill your every desire

Silhouette Desire delivers strong heroes, spirited heroines and stellar love stories.

Desire features your favorite authors, including

Diana Palmer, Annette Broadrick, Ann Major, Anne MacAllister and Cait London.

Passionate, powerful and provocative romances *guaranteed!*

For superlative authors, sensual stories and sexy heroes, choose Silhouette Desire.

Available at your favorite retail outlet.

Where love comes alive™

passionate powerful provocative love stories that fulfill your every desire

Silhouette ®

SPECIAL EDITION™

Emotional, compelling stories that capture the intensity of living, loving and creating a family in today's world.

Silhouette ®

Desire.

A highly passionate, emotionally powerful and always provocative read.

Silhouette ®

Where love comes alive™

Silhouette ®

INTIMATE MOMENTS™

A roller-coaster read that delivers romantic thrills in a world of suspense, adventure and more.

Silhouette Romance

From first love to forever, these love stories are for today's woman with traditional values.

Visit Silhouette at www.eHarlequin.com

SILGENINT